Manners That Matter

MANNERS
THAT MATTER
For People Under 21

by Dale Carlson & Dan Fitzgibbon

E. P. DUTTON ★ NEW YORK

Library of Congress Cataloging in Publication Data

Carlson, Dale Bick.   Manners that matter.

Summary: A handbook for dealing with all manners of
situations from dances and dinners to dating and
conversations.
1. Etiquette for youth.   [1. Etiquette]
I. Fitzgibbon, Dan.   II. Title.
BJ1857.C5C33   1983   395′.123   82-9761
ISBN 0-525-44008-9   AACR2

Published in the United States by E. P. Dutton, Inc.,
2 Park Avenue, New York, N.Y. 10016

Published simultaneously in Canada by Clarke,
Irwin & Company Limited, Toronto and Vancouver

Editor: Ann Durell   Designer: Claire Counihan

Printed in the U.S.A.   First Edition
10 9 8 7 6 5 4 3 2 1

I dedicate my much smaller part in
our first book together to Dan, whom
I love, and who is a wonderfully
talented writer.

Dale Carlson

I wish to express my love for Dale,
who lit the lamp of my creativity.

Dan Fitzgibbon

Contents

Introduction

This handbook to manners that matter was written to help
you get over, under, through, or around any awkward,
boring or unfamiliar situation from a formal dance to a formal dinner; from handling unwelcome party guests to a
weekend visit with your boyfriend and his family. It shows
you why manners aren't just mechanics to memorize, that
there is often some logic behind which fork you should use
for the salad and who gets introduced to whom. You'll also
find suggestions to bail you out of those embarrassing and
unexpected situations when you want to crawl under a rock
or sink through the floor. We'll talk about mastering it all—
from going out for the first time to your first romance to
your first breakup, from organizing your first party to your
first party problems. But the manners discussed apply to

more than just firsts; here are manners that will matter the rest of your life.

Following the simple suggestions in this book can make your life happier and make you more popular. Good manners are not only a natural expression of kindness and consideration; they are a passport to the affections of others. Did you ever notice how many popular girls and guys seem to have a natural grace and polite manners? Not "people pleasing," but a warm approach and style when socializing or just being with friends.

Sloppy or rude manners don't lead to popularity. They just turn people away or turn them off. People still get judged by their manners. First impressions still count a lot. Since not everybody has time to really get to know how wonderful you are underneath it all, chances are you will often be remembered by your manners instead.

If you ever want to test the power of manners, try a little experiment. Spend a couple of days being deliberately rude to those around you and watch what happens. Notice how your friends shift their feelings and attitudes toward you. Probably no one (except your parents) will ever demand that you "mind your manners." And it's unlikely that any attractive guy or girl will ever tell you how your sloppy manners or crude behavior quickly killed their interest in you. But, like it or not, your manners will have a lot to do with how you make it through life, at play and at work as well as in love.

Manners That Matter

Part ONE ★ BOYS AND GIRLS TOGETHER

Chapter 1 ★ Getting Together

Here are some simple suggestions to make going out easier, more relaxed and successful. Tact, common sense, and consideration for the other person are the basis for all good manners, particularly when it comes to the opposite sex.

Three Basic Ways To Ask Someone Out

in person
by telephone
in writing

The method you use will most likely depend on how friendly you are with the other person, how often you see this person and what you have planned (hamburger and movie, party, rock concert, prom, disco, football game).

3

Unless you are hosting a party, asking in person is probably the best approach. A phone call is also acceptable. If you are very shy, or the occasion is very special, a written note is fine. Whatever way you choose, be sure to do the asking yourself. Having a friend do the asking can lead to confusion or complications.

What To Say

Keep it simple. A friendly opening, such as, "Hello, I'm Jane/John" works just fine. Getting his or her attention shouldn't be a Broadway production.

Words that work Asking someone out, or hinting that you are available for the asking, may take courage. But it doesn't require either great wit or lots of smooth talk. Just be polite, pleasant and direct.

> EXAMPLES:
> "I've got two tickets for the basketball game Friday night, and I'd like you to go with me."
> "I'm having a Halloween party at my house on Saturday night, and I would like you to come."
> "Would you like to go out for a hamburger and a movie Sunday night?"

Have an alternative plan. There's always the chance the other person may already be going out or have other plans. Rather than be disappointed, why not suggest another time—it's perfectly acceptable.

EXAMPLES:

"I'm sorry you aren't free on Friday night. How about a movie on Sunday afternoon?"

"I'm sorry you can't come to the party. How about going with me to the state fairgrounds on Saturday the 10th?"

Be Specific.

It's both good manners and common sense to be specific about your plans:

> where you will be going (movie, dance, baseball game)
> when and what time (8:00 P.M. Friday)
> who will be with you (another couple, group)
> whether food will be served or ordered
> who is treating and/or providing transportation, especially if it's a group affair and/or Dutch treat

If it is a formal party or special event, be sure to inform the person so that the appropriate clothes can be worn. The more information he or she has, the fewer surprises and embarrassments there will be.

If Plans Change

No one likes to dress for a football game and be taken to a disco at the last moment. Let the person know about any changes in plans.

Call if you are going to be late. No one likes to be kept waiting without at least some warning.

Let the person know if you can't make it for any reason, and do it as soon as possible. Never just fail to show. It is rude and cruel to stand someone up.

A Few Last Getting-Together Hints

When someone asks you out, don't hedge with "Well I don't know, can we leave it open for a few days?" A definite yes or no as soon as possible is only courteous.

It's tactless and inconsiderate to ask someone out at the last minute. Friday night dates shouldn't be sought at 5:00 P.M. Friday. Assume the other person has an active social life, and ask well in advance of the day of the date.

Don't try to arrange two dates, an early one and a late one, for the same evening. Your popularity will benefit more from good manners than from the number of people you can squeeze into a day or night.

Since friendships and loyalties are important, think twice before asking out or going out with anyone who has recently been going out with one of your friends.

Plan to have a good time.

Now go have one.

Chapter 2 ★ Going-Out Manners That Matter

The Opening Scene

Be on time. Whether you are picking someone up at home or meeting on a street corner, it's bad manners to be late. If the person you're going out with picks you up at home, don't keep him or her waiting for twenty minutes.

Where to meet It's usual for a boy to meet a girl at her home, especially if they're going out for the first time. But it's perfectly okay, these days, for a girl to meet a boy at the event, or if the girl has the car, for her to pick him up.

Meeting the parents It is still considered good form for a young man to be introduced to a young woman's parents when he arrives to pick her up. A few moments' conversation makes her and her parents far more comfortable than a summons from a car horn outside.

Away We Go

What to say   Questions are always a good way to break the ice and get to know another person.

>EXAMPLES:
>
>What do you like in the way of sports, music, dancing, books, movies, records, food, clothes, whatever?
>
>How do you feel about the future, goals, family life, your relatives, school, work, war, peace, or the Chinese?

Do show a genuine interest in the other person and his or her answers. Don't be afraid to be a good listener.

Introduce your date to others.   As mentioned in the chapter on introductions (pages 31–38), always introduce the person you're with, whether you're at a party or dance, or you happen to meet others you know on the street.

Stay with your date.   Wandering off with the guys or the girls and leaving the person you're with to shift for herself or himself is bad form. If both of you know most of the people at a party or dance and agree ahead of time about dancing or spending time with others, the situation takes care of itself. But long absences aren't too welcome, particularly if he or she isn't very well acquainted with the others at the dance or party. Dinner, theater, movie, or spectator sports events have a built-in requirement for the couple to stay together, but do be equally attentive at larger gatherings.

Clinging The opposite form of behavior can also be unattractive. Do leave your partner some conversational, breathing, dancing room at a party. Consistent close contact (clinging), hovering, overprotectiveness, or possessiveness can be uncomfortable for everyone.

Flirting and carrying on with others of the opposite sex while on a date (especially a first date) is tactless and inconsiderate. If someone else interests you, that's fine. But save the flirting for another day.

If you like the person you're with, say so. Appreciation is fun for everybody. Tell him or her how you feel—in any one of a dozen ways.

> EXAMPLES:
> "I really like your smile; it's so warm and friendly."
> "I like your taste in clothes, especially what you're wearing tonight."
> "I'm very happy you asked me out."

Some quiet compliments and warm words can make going out more enjoyable—and they are always appropriate.

Parting

Home safe means just that.   Keep in mind that you made a round-trip agreement. Don't leave a girl at the corner of the block—escort her right to her door. If you are a girl and you agreed to drive him home, the same courtesy holds.

Observe the curfew.   If either of your parents has set a curfew, honor it. If necessary, call for an extension, and try to call early. Parents also have rights.

If you are going out with another couple in their car, you have the right to accept or reject any lovers' lane detour on the way home. Ask to be dropped off if you wish. Don't feel trapped.

Too hot to handle   If your date suddenly turns into Mr. Passion Plus at the end of the evening, be direct and clear about what it is you *don't* want. If he ignores you and becomes too aggressive, it's best to leave him, step out of the car, or make other arrangements to get home. Be firm. Again, don't feel trapped.

Kissing and telling sometimes backfires. You may want to do an instant replay with your friends, but respect the other person's privacy.

Be careful of criticism.   No one likes it.

Say thank you.   Everyone loves to hear it.

Chapter 3 ★ Going Places

Going out is a lot more fun if you know what you're doing. Learn a few special codes of behavior, and the whole world of dining and entertaining is your own party! Here's how to cope, whether you go to a local restaurant, to a school dance, or to the opera.

Who Pays for What?

Traditionally when going out, men have paid the expenses for such things as movies, dances, dinner at a restaurant or a ball game. However, customs are changing, and many young women are paying their own way right from the beginning. Although some young men may prefer to pay the expenses of the first few evenings, there are no established rules. But it might be helpful to keep the following in mind:

When you invite someone out, be absolutely clear about who is paying the expenses. If you are planning to cover all the expenses yourself, be sure you communicate this fact.

If your intention is that each of you pay your own way, the best way to avoid confusion (and maybe resentment) is to be specific in your invitation.

If you are being invited out and it's not clear who is paying for what, don't be timid: Ask.

Whenever the circumstances are vague or you forget to ask, it's wise to carry enough money so you can pay your own expenses.

If you have been invited out on a pay-your-own-way basis and you are short of money—but very much want to go—share your situation with the other person. You might be pleasantly surprised to learn that the inviter is willing to pay your way.

Some young men had been taught a very rigid code and may have trouble when their partner tries to pay all or some of the expenses. To avoid damaged pride, be sure to discuss it in advance.

When a group of unattached people attend a movie or concert, each should plan to pay his or her own way. And the presence of someone's parents doesn't necessarily mean that you will get a free ride. If you are uncertain about who will be paying, ask!

Restaurants and Eating Out

A mark of good manners is never to be rude or call undue attention to yourself. This is particularly important when dining out. Although most of your dining out will probably consist of informal meals or snacks at McDonald's or the local pizza parlor, it helps to be prepared and knowledgeable about the customs and procedures of more formal dining.

The host　The person who does the inviting is also responsible for making any reservations that might be necessary. She or he should also inquire about any dress code (some restaurants require a shirt, tie and jacket, or at least a jacket.) These can often be borrowed from the restaurant; ask about it.

Checkroom　Some restaurants and discos have checkrooms. Men are generally expected to check their coats; women have the option of checking theirs or taking them to the table. Checkroom attendants generally expect to be tipped for their services. Be prepared to do so except when you see the notice NO TIPPING ALLOWED.

Who follows whom?　If you have made reservations in advance, give the name and size of your party to whoever greets you. If the restaurant has a captain, maître d'hôtel or hostess, that person will seat you. When being escorted to your table, the women follow the captain or hostess, and the men follow the women. If the captain pulls out one of the chairs at the table, one of the women should be seated there. The captain or hostess is the person responsible for ensuring that you receive good service, whatever you order, and for filling any special requests.

If you are dining at a restaurant where there is no captain or hostess, whoever is the host of the party leads the way and selects a table that is agreeable to all.

Seating arrangements   How to arrange your seating if you are a party of three or more is optional. When there are two or more couples, the women generally sit opposite each other. When arriving at the table, the man holds the chair for the woman. He also helps her take off her coat. If the restaurant has booth seating, women sit on the inside.

The menu   There are two different ways to order:

A la carte   You pay for each dish separately. The price is listed next to each item. This is more expensive than *table d'hôte.*

Table d'hôte   You will be charged a single price for the complete meal, but you may order extra or side dishes separately if you wish. If you are uncertain about what food or side dishes are included in the price, don't hesitate to ask. Waiters are accustomed to such inquiries. The menu will list a group of appetizers, soups, entrées (main courses), salads, vegetables, and desserts. The total price of the meal will appear next to the entrée. *Prix fixe* is like table d'hôte.

The service   If, for some reason, the service is very slow or the waiter rude, inform the captain or hostess. However, you or your party should not reciprocate with rude actions such as shouting or whistling for your waiter, snapping your fingers or banging a glass to get attention. Bad manners are not the answer to poor service.

Group behavior Try to avoid anything such as loud, noisy conversation that will disturb the other patrons. They have the right to a quiet enjoyment of their meal. Pot smoking, yelling to friends across the restaurant or playing practical jokes are out. The pocketing of ashtrays, glassware or utensils as souvenirs is really petty theft—not part of dining out.

Wrong orders or bad food Dining out can be expensive. And since you are paying for it, you are entitled to get what you ordered: good food cooked the way you asked for it. If the food served is not what you ordered (the steak is rare and you asked for well done, you ordered spinach and were served peas), don't hesitate to inform the waiter or hostess. Be courteous but firm.

The bill and tipping If you are paying, be sure to bring more than you expect to need—especially if it is an expensive place to eat. If you are being treated, bring some cash along just in case. It's no fun spending your entire meal worrying whether you have enough money or, worse yet, choosing an entrée you don't like just because it is the least expensive item on the menu.

Customarily, the host requests the bill after everyone has finished eating. Always check the addition on the bill for mistakes—it's your money. If you are in a group and each couple is paying their own bill, ask for separate checks at the time you order. Remember, also, that there are some-times charges you didn't expect. For example, most states levy a tax that can amount to 6, 7, or even 8 percent of your bill. If the restaurant has entertainment, there may be a cover charge (extra fee) for this or an admission charge.

The amount you tip may vary depending on the type of restaurant and the extent of the service. Generally, an amount equal to 15 percent of the bill (before tax) is quite acceptable. If you are somewhat dissatisfied with the ser-vice (not the taste of the food), you may leave a reduced tip. Failing to leave any tip or leaving only pennies is too unfair and should be avoided. If the meal is paid for with a credit card, the tip is added to the bottom of the slip.

Proms, Dances and Discotheques

Who pays? Tickets for the evening are usually paid for by whoever does the inviting unless a Dutch treat has been agreed on. Some events, like proms, call for advance ticket buying, while others, such as discos, are just paid for at the door or at your table before you leave.

When to bring flowers The decision to bring a cor-sage will depend on the fashion of the time and the wom-an's taste. For proms and other formal dances, it's best to ask the woman what her feelings are about flowers. If she wants flowers, do be sure to ask about the color (to match her dress). And if you are a woman, and you want a cor-sage, keep in mind, please, the pocketbook of your escort.

Shall we dance? Whether the dance is formal or semiformal, there are a few customs that should be observed.

If there is a specific hostess, the men are expected to ask her to dance as a gesture of respect and recognition of her hospitality.

If you go in a group of two or more couples, the men are expected to dance with each other's dates.

The first and last dance are traditionally danced with the person you came with.

Single men may cut in on a dancing couple at many dances. Although at some discotheques and night clubs, especially for young people, cutting in on strangers is permitted, do be sure of the customs of the place. To cut in, tap the shoulder of the woman's dancing partner and ask "May I cut in?" Dance until the next musical break, or until someone else cuts in. In neither sex is it polite to strand the other person in the middle of the music or the dance floor.

Theater, Movies and Concerts

Please be seated. If an usher shows you to your seats, the women follow the usher, the men follow the women. Men generally sit closest to the aisle. If there are two couples, the women sit next to each other between the men. (These rules are constantly ignored, but you might as well know them.)

There may be strict rules about late seating at a concert, so plan to arrive in good time.

When others are trying to get by you to their seats, always stand and, if possible, push your seat back. Don't stay seated, as it makes passage difficult and awkward. Nor is it good form to leave before the performance ends just to avoid the rush.

Needless to say, at-home television manners are seldom popular in public. Crunching, crackling candy paper, or exchanging remarks, even in whispers, disturbs the pleasure of others. If you are disturbed by someone's bad manners, it is perfectly proper to say, "Please be quiet. I can't hear." If the noise continues, call an usher.

Do applaud or cheer with the rest of the audience. Random appreciation only disturbs the performers and the rest of the audience.

Sports and Other Public Events

Don't get in everybody else's way too often by jumping up and down. Do observe yells of "Down in front."

It's easy to get separated or lost in a large crowd. Just in case, be sure you suggest a meeting place for after the event. Also note where you are sitting, where the car is parked, and where you can get a bus or other transportation if necessary.

Public Beaches, Amusement Parks, Outdoor Concerts

Observe the preceding rules about getting separated.

Make sure you have extra money in case you have to get yourself home.

Remember also: Littering and noise pollution (no loud playing or radios—bring earplugs or earphones if your transistor radio has much volume) are a public nuisance as well as bad manners.

Chapter 4 ★ Going-Steady Manners

Sometimes when two people agree to be a twosome, strange things begin to happen. What was once common courtesy may become uncommon. What started out as familiarity can turn into just sloppy manners or inconsiderate behavior. Showing up late and taking your steady for granted may begin to replace punctuality and total devotion. Your friends and relatives also require consideration and attention, even if your main focus is elsewhere. What follows are some basic guidelines to help you keep everyone and everything in balance.

Everyday Affairs

Most couples try to establish some workable principles that guide their day-to-day behavior and express their concern for each other. Some reasonable suggestions might include:

Make it a joint decision when planning time together. Show consideration for your partner's likes and dislikes. Remember—there are *two* people in an *us*.

Committing your partner to a party or dance before clearing it with her or him is pretty inconsiderate. When faced with the situation of suddenly being invited somewhere, it's best to say, "It sounds fine to me, but let me check with Sue and be sure she hasn't made other plans." It's not a sign of weakness to check with your steady—it's good manners.

Monopolizing the other one's time can be selfish and inconsiderate. Playing "Siamese twin" can put a strain on your partner and your relationship. Give the other person breathing room. You can't be all things to that special person, nor can that person be everything to you. Both of you need to grow and build and be.

Dominating a conversation or speaking on behalf of your steady can prove particularly annoying and rude. Unless you have been appointed official spokesman, it's best to let your partner express his or her own thoughts.

Getting sloppy in personal appearance or continuously arriving late can be signals that you are taking your partner for granted. Try to show the same courtesies that you enjoy receiving.

Money Matters

Going steady generally involves a good bit of caring and sharing. It's only natural that this approach should extend to how you handle entertainment expenses. Although there are no set rules or laws about who will pay what expenses, the following suggestions might lead to a happier relationship.

Couples should make an effort to discuss the expense-sharing issue. Things left unsaid can lead to confusion, hurt feelings, and resentments.

Sharing equally is an ideal to strive for, but each person's resources should be considered. If one person has a part-time job or a generous allowance and the other isn't so fortunate, common sense suggests that the one with more will carry most of the expenses.

If both partners have limited resources, share and share alike is probably the most equitable arrangement.

Whatever your solution is, try not to keep score or be too rigid about the way you handle the expenses. People have strange attitudes about money, so do keep things in perspective.

When in doubt, it's probably best that you contribute more than your share. After all, it's only money!

Other People Still Count.

In any good relationship, the courtesy and consideration that you show to others is just as important as the respect you show each other. While working out the give-and-take elements of your partnership, try not to overlook these essential courtesies to friends and family.

The family is a private unit. If your steady will be visiting you, notify the rest of your family in advance. A little advance warning can prevent inconvenience, embarrassing moments, and the short tempers that go with feeling invaded.

Be sure that meal invitations are cleared in advance. Don't leave your parents wondering whether you will be bringing home a guest.

If you spend considerable time at your steady's home, it's only fair to offer to help with small chores such as running errands, helping to prepare a meal, or helping to clean up afterward.

In your efforts to be considerate of others, you and your steady should remember that the home you are in belongs to a *whole* family, not just the two of you.

Some privacy please Most couples that are going steady enjoy their moments of privacy. Talk to your brothers and sisters, parents, or friends about your wishes. Don't just assume people will stay out of your way. Share your needs and avoid hurt feelings. "Please don't come in" ahead of time works better than "Get out of here!" after the fact.

Try not to flaunt it. For some peculiar reason there are those couples who feel that it is important to go public and flaunt their togetherness and intimacy. Some of their behavior may be classified as rude or even offensive. Certainly it is often at least in bad taste. A little prudent behavior might save you some painful experiences.

Watch the public displays of affection. Some people think they're invisible. They're not. Suggestion: Keep the embraces short, sweet, and simple. The ten-minute clutch is generally thought ill-mannered.

Although it's great to share your feelings with your close

friends, kissing and telling—in detail—can be thoughtless.

Suggestion: Perhaps the intimate details of your romance are best left for your diary or personal memories, rather than the ears of friends or the locker-room gang.

Your friends should not be abruptly deserted during a budding romance. They can feel hurt and left out. Also, romances tend to come and go, but good friends remain. Suggestion: Try for some balance in your relationships with others. Do keep in touch with friends and buddies. Dropping out of sight or ignoring good friends tops the list of poor romantic manners.

Chapter 5 ★ The Art of Saying No and Taking No

This is a difficult world, and one of the things we eventually have to learn about is the art of saying no and taking no. Saying no won't make you the most unpopular person at school, and having someone say no to you doesn't mean that you are unloved, unwanted, or a reject. If you think about it, you will probably realize that what is behind another person's no is just about the same thing that is behind your no. Nothing lethal (unless it's one of those "No, absolutely not, get out of my life" numbers). Just "I happen to be busy, but that doesn't mean you aren't terrific" is all most no's are about.

Nobody Likes To Say No.

No may be one of the most unpopular words in the dictionary, but saying it doesn't make you unpopular. It may take some courage and a deep breath to force the word out, but saying exactly what you mean shows your respect for the other person. What most people don't always understand is that yes and no have a lot to do with being courteous, considerate, and sensitive to the feelings of others. Saying yes when you mean no can be misleading, hurtful, and just bad manners. It's always better to say "I don't know" or "No" at first than to say "Yes" and then let someone down by changing to "No" later on.

When to say no   There are two very important occasions when you should say no:

> when you really feel like it, for whatever the reason
> when it seems appropriate and courteous

> EXAMPLE:
> You have been asked out by a boy who has been going out with a close friend of yours. Out of consideration for your girlfriend and her feelings, you might decline to go out—at least until you talk it over with her.

The soft touch   There's a lot of truth to the statement, it's not so much *what* you say as *how* you say it. It's particularly helpful to keep this in mind when you have to tell someone no. Gentleness can blunt the sharp edges of a "No."

> EXAMPLES:
> You can smile when you say no. You don't have to look grim when you say the word.

Add the words "Thank you" or maybe "That's very kind of you, but no thanks."

Use another word or phrase that's a little softer and conveys the same meaning, such as, "Thanks for asking, but I've made other plans" or "I appreciate your interest, but I have a heavy schedule."

It's really okay to be friendly and pleasant when you say no. So many people feel so guilty saying no, they say it unpleasantly and hurt others' feelings.

Afraid to say no   If you feel intimidated or confused about how to say no or decline an invitation, just remember you aren't doing anyone a favor by agreeing to do something you don't want to do. It's more polite to bear the discomfort of saying no for a few moments than to go through with something ungraciously, grumbling all the way. It's important to know yourself what it is you feel about the person who is asking or inviting, and then to make it clear by the way you say no. If you really mean no altogether, make that no friendly but firm. But if you want to leave the door open for future consideration, then let the person know that, too, with a simple "Please ask me again" or "Perhaps some other time." And smile!

The persistent ones   Every once in a while, you will encounter the kind of person who does not understand the meaning of the word *no*. When you phrase the words softly, the persistent one completely ignores your response. Maybe the persistent one even gets aggressive or demanding.

Probably the best way to deal with this kind of person is to:

Deliver a firm no, with whatever other plain English you feel is essential.

Communicate how you feel quietly and without ridiculing the other person or making a scene—but repeat several times that you really aren't going to say yes.

If it all gets too uncomfortable, ask for someone else's help.

Nobody Likes Receiving a No.

Just as there are two sides to a coin, there are also those occasions when a response to you will be no. It may even be delivered with more intensity or indifference than you ever expected. A few thoughts to keep in mind when a no arrives:

Accepting a no graciously is one of the few things more difficult than saying no. No one likes to be turned down—it smarts and it stings—especially when it's important to you. Remember:

—It's poor form to turn bitter and snap at the person saying no.

—If you have the right to say no, so does everyone else.

Plotting the social assassination of someone who declined your invitation is a form of retaliation that's not only bad manners, but often backfires on your own reputation.

Not everyone will see the magic in you, just as you

don't always see the magic in those around you. You don't like everyone. Why should everyone like you?

Acceptance of the word *no* takes practice. A no doesn't diminish who you are unless you let it by reacting with bad manners.

Breaking Up—The Big No

There are those occasions when you may find yourself on the receiving end of a big no—and it hurts deeply. When a romance turns sour, good manners are given the true test. No matter how things turn out, you'll think better of yourself if you behave well. Here are a few simple suggestions for keeping your dignity intact.

Don't just let the relationship deteriorate slowly because you are afraid to hurt the other person's feelings. If the magic is gone, deal with it directly and honestly. It will hurt less than the frustration of a slow breakup. And don't just return a ring by mail or slip a "good-bye" note into one of the person's books. Explain your feelings face to face as best you can.

Do your best to avoid indulging in public denunciation of your former partner. The "I'll tell the world how miserable you are" approach merely highlights your own bad form. Try to share your feelings only with your family and close friends.

If there is property involved (a class ring maybe), return it. The same is true for personal things you may have borrowed (records, tapes, books, a sweater). Deliver them directly or drop them off at the other person's home.

Involving your friends as message carriers or partisans can try their loyalty. If there are some loose ends or incomplete issues between you, handle these yourself, not through a third person.

It's also poor form to toss insults at or stonewall your former steady, especially among a group of common friends. If you're feeling awfully tender, try to avoid being in the same place at the same time for a while. But displays of rudeness don't cause hurt feelings to disappear, and if the other person retaliates, you may end up feeling worse.

Try holding your chin up in public, having a good cry in private, and remembering that you have to let go of one thing for something even better to happen!

Part TWO ★
THE BEST
OF MANNERS

Chapter 6 ★ Introductions

The way you introduce yourself can make a lasting impression. A mumble, a limp handshake, and people forget you fast. A courteous introduction of yourself, a polite acknowledgment of others, and people will want to know you better.

Introducing your family and friends to others is easy with a little practice.

Basic Rules of Introduction

1. A *man* is always introduced to a *woman.*

   EXAMPLE:

   "Jane, may I introduce Bob Hood."

31

2. A *young* person is always introduced to an *older* person.

EXAMPLE:

"Mrs. Hendrick, I would like you to meet Janet King."

3. *Less* distinguished persons are introduced to *more* socially prominent individuals.

EXAMPLES:

"Doctor Carlson, I would like you to meet my sister Patricia."

"Bishop Brown, this is my brother Jonathan."

These three basic rules will become automatic with practice. And remember, the easiest and friendliest forms of introduction will generally serve you best in a world that has become less formal. For instance:

When introducing a young couple, it is perfectly all right to use their first names, "Sue and Frank Marshall," rather than the more formal "Mr. and Mrs. Marshall."

Introductions don't have to be elaborate in wording either. Most often they consist of short, friendly phrases such as:

"I would like you to meet . . ."
"This is . . ."
"Have you met . . . ?"

Many people use a short description when making an introduction. This tactic helps promote an opening conversation.

EXAMPLES:

"Professor Simmons, I would like you to meet the captain of our basketball team, Tom Jackson."
"Sue, this is my cousin from California, Linda."

When To Introduce

The general rule is that an introduction is in order whenever two unknown individuals meet while one is accompanied by a friend.

EXAMPLE:

Jack and Jill bump into Jack's cousin when leaving a movie. Jack introduces his cousin to Jill.

This same rule should govern your behavior if you are walking with a few friends (or your parents) and stop to chat with one or more persons unknown to your friends (or parents).

The introductions may take a little time, but they are still pretty essential to everyone's comfort.

EXAMPLES:

"Lisa, I would like you to meet Bill and his brother Fred."
"Mom and Dad, these are my classmates Laura, Kathy, and Anne."

It is considered rude and unkind to stop and greet others but fail to introduce those accompanying you. Certainly no one gets any fun out of being ignored, even if it's only a chance meeting.

A last note: When you are in doubt about whether people already know each other, introduce them anyway.

Introducing Yourself

Fortunately, life is not as "proper" as it was fifty years ago, and no one needs to wait for a formal introduction. Whenever you are in a situation where the host or hostess can't handle all the introductions, simply introduce yourself. At a large party, a church function, or a school dance, all you need to do is walk up to any person (or persons) you wish to meet and say something informal.

> EXAMPLES:
>
> "Hello, I'm Nancy Summers; I'm visiting with Dr. Brown and his family."
> "Hi, I'm Don Johnson, the new ski instructor."

It can be helpful to the other person if you add a little bit of history about yourself as in the preceding examples. If you already know the person's name but you doubt the person knows you, it's easy to lead off with, "Hello, Mrs. Worth. I'm Jeff Spender, a friend of your son Dan's."

Introducing Others

One-to-one introductions The most common introduction is one involving you, someone accompanying you, and a friend, relative, or acquaintance that you meet. The three basic rules apply here.

1. Introduce the man to the woman: "Barbara, I would like you to meet Ted Baxter."
2. A young person is introduced to an older person: "Mrs. Amherst, this is Jim Tyler, our new school reporter."
3. The less distinguished person is introduced to the prominent individual: "Doctor Jones, this is my cousin Mary from Florida."

Introducing one to a group Introductions to a group of people—usually at a party or social function—take a bit more time but aren't difficult. Just follow these simple guidelines.

In a very large crowd, simply introduce your friend to the host/hostess and those people near you when you enter (assuming you know them). Or you may selectively introduce the person accompanying you to some special friends at the party or gathering. If the gathering is informal, first names will do fine. To ensure that you have the attention and interest of the others, it's best to name them first and then your companion.

EXAMPLE:

"Allen, Phil, Sam, and Harry, this is my cousin Chuck from New York."

Again, when possible, give a little opening history.

Simple courtesy dictates that you don't just whisk your companion into the middle of the group of party and leave him or her stranded. This can be especially painful for someone who doesn't know anyone else. Break the ice with some introductions.

Introducing couples to couples The rules to follow here are quite simple. They are useful not only for parties or just walking around, but for school functions, to which so many people seem to come in pairs.

Introduce the younger couple to the older couple.

Introduce the less prominent couple to the more distinguished or honored couple. (This may depend on the circumstances. At school, the more honored couple may be the principal and his wife; at church, the pastor and his wife; at other times, your parents.)

Among young couples, first names are generally used. However, introducing a young couple to an elderly couple may call for the use of the more formal *Mr.* and *Mrs.*

EXAMPLES:

"Sue and Frank, I would like you to meet Kay and Ron."

"Mr. and Mrs. Graves, this is Melissa and her friend Mark."

Special introductions In those situations when you are introducing your parents or relatives to a friend or acquaintance, the accepted procedure is to mention the friend or acquaintance first.

EXAMPLES:

"Lorna, this is my mother and father."

"Ellen, I would like you to meet my cousin Agnes."

Try to avoid introducing your parents by their first names. It's not considered proper.

Stepparents can sometimes cause a bit of confusion as

they may have a different last name. An easy way to handle the introduction is: "Mildred, this is my stepfather, Mr. Williams."

Your date's parents should be addressed as Mr. and Mrs. The formal address should be used unless they specifically invite you to call them by their first names.

Teachers and employers are normally referred to in a formal manner.

> EXAMPLES:
>
> "Mr. Gordon (teacher), this is my brother Frank."
> "Mr. Sanders (store owner and boss), I would like you to meet my friend Philip."

Your Response to an Introduction

When you have been introduced to someone, the most common and correct response is a friendly "Hello." You may choose to include their names: "Hello, Maureen." The more formal response is "How do you do, Mrs. James?" Other acceptable responses include "I'm very glad to meet you" and "It's a pleasure to meet you."

Men traditionally shake hands when they meet. Women may or may not offer their hands. Young boys and girls shake hands with adults; young men and women, with their elders.

Points To Keep in Mind

> When shaking hands, do so with a firm grasp.
>
> Should you forget the name of a person you are expected to introduce, try the simple tactic, "Have you

two met?'' It's a clear signal that you have forgotten the name. An alert person will quickly save the scene by saying, "Hello, I'm Dorothy Kelly." Whenever you are in a situation where you have forgotten the name and the preceding tactic doesn't work, you will have to admit that you have forgotten the name and ask for it: "'I'm sorry, just for the moment I've forgotten your name" or "I'm sorry, I'm just awful with names" or "I'm so embarrassed; I don't remember your name." Don't try to cover up or evade the introduction. A forgotten name is a pretty common incident.

If you didn't catch the name, simply say, "I'm sorry; I didn't hear your name."

When introducing yourself to someone who may have forgotten who you are, avoid the challenge, "You don't remember me." Just introduce yourself in the conventional manner and mention where you previously met or saw the other person.

And now that you're properly introduced, it's probably time to eat. Table manners are next!

Chapter 7 ★ Table Manners

Your knowledge of good table manners will allow you to relax and enjoy eating with others. Instead of feeling anxious about making a mistake or a mess, you can concentrate on the pleasures of good food and good company. Here are the basic customs, a step-by-step guide to acquaint you with the primary rules of the table.

The Setting

Although the placement of the different pieces of silverware, plates and glassware may appear to be a complex mystery—it's all pretty simple. If you are asked to help set the table, don't panic. Just keep in mind the following guidelines.

Silverware For most meals, the required silverware will consist of a knife, fork and spoon placed in the following manner.

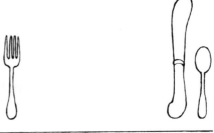

If the meal is more elaborate or formal, the silverware may include a soup spoon, a dessert spoon, salad fork and regular fork. Placement follows use. When eating, you start with your soup, then you eat your salad and, finally, your main course. The utensils to be used first are placed on the outside, as shown below. At a meal, each person begins with the outside utensils and works his or her way in.

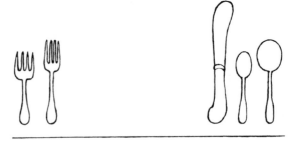

Dishes In addition to the plate for the main course, the table setting may include the following: a bread and butter plate, a salad plate or some other side dish. The customary placement is to the left of your main dish, as shown at the top of page 41.

Glassware For most meals, a single glass is placed at the top right of your place setting, as in the picture above. On special occasions, a water goblet and a wineglass may be used. Placement of these glassware items is shown in the following illustration.

Napkins are generally folded and placed on the left side of the setting. However, you may find a fancy "cocked hat" napkin placed in the middle of the dinner plate. That's all right too!

Like so many other things in this world, there are no absolute, cut-in-stone rules for table settings. The preceding description represents a nice, workable approach. Don't be upset if someone else was brought up with different rules. Remember, in some countries it is acceptable to eat with one's fingers; in many cultures food is pushed into the mouth while holding the plate or bowl to the lips.

Serving and Eating

During the serving and eating of the meal, the most common rules to keep in mind deal with:

Reaching It's not polite to reach across another person or half the table. When something is out of reach, ask the person nearest to it: "Mr. Hawks, would you please pass the salt?"

Helping yourself At many meals, the *family style* of dining is used. Each person serves herself or himself as the plates of food are passed around the table. If you are not sure how much food to take, observe how much the host or hostess has on his or her plate.

At some parties and larger gatherings, the *buffet style* of dining is preferred. The food is arranged in large serving trays or dishes at a central table. This self-service table will also contain a stock of plates, silverware and napkins. The guests are expected to gather up their own place settings, fill their plates with whatever they desire, and find a spot to sit and eat. Sometimes this can be a bit of a juggling act, and a three-armed person has a definite advantage. If you are new at it, just watch how others do it. Caution: A heaping serving tray of your favorite food may tempt you to overload your plate, so be considerate of others. Give everyone a fair chance. Serve yourself a reasonable amount at the initial serving.

Being served by a waiter or maid When being served, keep in mind that all of your food will be served to you from your left side and empty plates will be removed from your right side.

Second helping In family-style and buffet dining, you are expected to help yourself to seconds. Where food is being served to you by the hosts, you pass your plate *with* your knife and fork on the plate. Don't rest your utensils on the table while you are eating. If you are using your knife to cut meat, it should rest on your plate when not in use.

Special servings When serving yourself butter, jam, sauce, and so forth from dishes on the table, use the butter knife, spoon, or ladle that comes with the serving dish, not your own.

Foods you dislike If the main course or primary food is a dish that you don't like or can't eat, the courteous thing to do is to accept the serving anyway. If it is home-style service, take a small portion and concentrate on the other foods. All other foods such as vegetables, soup, or salad may be refused (politely) if you don't like the partic-ular food. Do *not* upset someone else's pleasure at dinner by discussing your distaste.

The pusher Even small children are discouraged from using their fingers as pushers. For anyone old enough to be at a table, fingers are forbidden. Your knife or a piece of bread are the only acceptable pushers for slippery or stubborn food.

Bread and butter The important thing to remember about bread and butter is never to butter a whole piece of bread. Break off a small piece at a time, butter it, and break off another. Each roll or slice of bread should be broken into at least two or three pieces.

Difficult foods Every once in a while you may find yourself staring at one of those foods or dishes that you aren't sure just how to eat—such as fried chicken, baked lobster, oysters on the half shell or artichokes. Here are some tips that can take the struggle or uncertainty out of your meal.

Chicken and other fowl At a formal dinner, always use a knife and fork. At home, or at informal dinners, you may use your fingers.

Lobster It may be funny looking, but it is fairly easy to eat. Most cooks and restaurants cut open the lobster on the underside from chest to tail. All you need do is lift out the meat with a fork (if available, a small pointed lobster fork is best) and dip each piece in melted butter for added taste. For the claws and legs you will need to use the nutcracker that will be provided. Crack much as you would a nut and use a fork to remove the lobster meat. Eating a lobster is a bit messy for everyone—that's why restaurants usually supply you with a huge napkin and a spare plate for the shell pieces.

Artichokes You first eat the base of each artichoke leaf and then the pulpy central heart. Each leaf is removed with your fingers, and the base of the leaf (which has a small amount of pulp) is dipped into melted butter. Most of each leaf is discarded. The pulpy heart is cut up and eaten with your knife and fork (pieces dipped in butter).

Spaghetti Simply twirl the spaghetti around your fork, using a large spoon for support if you have one. It's also acceptable to rest the tines of your fork on the plate.

Melons A watermelon can be a finger food only on picnics. Otherwise, it is eaten with a fork or fork and knife. Melons that are served cut in half are generally eaten with a spoon. Those served in sections can be eaten with a knife and fork or spoon.

Corn and pizza Corn on the cob and slices of pizza are delicious foods that can be eaten with your fingers. Pizza is more manageable if you fold it in half and tuck in the point.

Soup Be sure to spoon the soup away from you, not toward you. If you must tip the bowl, tip the bowl away from you as well. If clear broth is served to you in a cup, you may if you wish drink it directly from the cup.

Oysters on the half shell Simply stab the oyster meat with your fork, dip the meat into whatever sauce is being used and then down the oyster.

Table Mishaps

Just about everyone has been confronted with a problem or embarrassing moment while eating. Here are the more common incidents and some commonsense ways to handle them.

Taking food out of your mouth If you bite into a piece of fat, skin, gristle, or spoiled food, simply tongue it back onto your fork or spoon and place it on the edge of your plate. Don't remove the food with your fingers. If a bit of food is stuck between your teeth, wait till the end of the meal and then retire to the bathroom to pry it out. If it's really bothering you during the meal, excuse yourself and go remedy the problem. Picking at your teeth anytime during a meal or in public isn't a popular act.

Hot food or choking When a bit of food is sizzling hot in your mouth, reach for the water or another beverage and take a swallow. If some food lodges in your throat or windpipe causing you to choke, again try water or place your napkin over your mouth while you try to cough it up, dislodge it, or swallow it.

Spilled food It happens to all of us. If you spill the food on the tablecloth, simply scoop it up with a knife or spoon and dab up any stain with a little water, using your napkin. If the mishap is a larger one (food spilled on the floor, gravy all over the buffet table), quickly alert the hostess, apologize and offer to clean it up under her direction. Should you drop a knife or fork on the floor, retrieve it and set it aside, then ask for a replacement.

Sneezing or coughing Merely turn your head away and cover your mouth or nose with a napkin. If it is a sustained bout of sneezing or coughing, excuse yourself from the table.

General Table Rules

Although it isn't required or expected in everyday dining, at formal or special dinners it is customary for the man to hold the chair for the woman on his right (and then, if necessary, for the woman on his left).

Napkins should remain in your lap. When you use a napkin, blot your mouth: Don't scrub it. Your napkin is laid, not crumpled or folded, on the table *after* the hostess has laid hers on the table as a signal that the meal is over.

Posture is important. It's best not to slouch or sprawl your arms all over the table. You may rest your elbows or forearms on the table, but not while you are eating. When eating, bring the food up to your mouth, not your mouth down to your food. You needn't sit stiffly at the table, but remember, a relaxed posture does not mean tilting your chair.

Begin eating only after everyone is served at gatherings of six or less people. For larger groups, it is customary to start eating after three or four people have been served.

When you are finished with the main course, your knife and fork should be placed beside each other on the plate, diagonally from upper left to lower right.

Don't talk with food in your mouth—EVER!

Don't take liquid in your mouth *with* your food to wash it down.

Don't push your plate away or otherwise rearrange your dishes from their setting position when you have finished eating.

Don't engage in gory or distasteful conversation (vivisection, operations, accidents, animal slaughter) while eating.

Don't comb your hair, apply makeup, or groom yourself at the table.

Don't smoke during the meal unless others do. If there are no ashtrays on the table, perhaps there is a reason. If the urge to smoke is compelling, at least wait until everyone is finished eating. Smoking while people are eating makes some people lose their appetite. So does snuffing out a cigarette in a fried egg or other food.

All's Well That Ends Well.

A few final words to end the meal:

The hostess will usually signal the end of the meal by placing her napkin on the table. Follow her example.

All people appreciate compliments. Expressing appreciation of the food and the occasion is a gracious finishing touch!

Chapter 8 ★ What To Wear and When

One of the ways people express themselves is in the clothes they wear. But as with your manners, your clothes are also one of the ways others judge you. So you'll want to be sure your clothes *express* you rather than *condemn* you.

In everyday living, people wear pretty much what they like, what others are wearing, what suits them. However, there are some occasions and events for which there is a code for dressing. Just as an evening dress doesn't belong at a picnic, jeans don't belong at proms, weddings or funerals. For special occasions, the important word is *appropriate*. So here we'll talk about appropriate dress for those special occasions, and what is sensible and acceptable, so you won't stick out like a sore thumb. We will also discuss everyday wear and the importance of being comfortable with your clothing selections.

Everyday Wear

Whether at a movie, in a classroom or at a sporting event, your clothing choices are fairly simple. You can either dress like most of the crowd or dress like none of the crowd, depending on how you feel (and perhaps on how much courage or flair you have).

One general principle you might consider, however, is to try to look reasonably neat and clean. Well-groomed hair and nails are essential. A shirt and jeans may be your everyday outfit—but they don't have to be soiled or torn. Rumpled clothes that give the impression you spent the last twenty minutes being tumble-dried won't enhance your social standing. And clothes that have had too much mileage detract from your sparkling personality. You may favor the counterculture life-style or the look of the punk rock set. It's fine to enjoy your own choice of style. Sometimes, however, one's method of dress can be too extreme or provocative for comfort.

Here are a few guidelines that you might at least think about.

Most everyone likes attention, but very, very tight clothes, whether worn innocently or with intent, can earn you some negative attention—especially at a church or old folks' gathering.

If you aren't happy with the state of the world, do tell people about it. But try to refrain from having your favorite T-shirt carry a "tough language" message.

The older generations tend to wince and scowl a lot when they see the younger set wearing garish colors, chrome-studded leather jackets or World War II fatigues at family get-togethers. It doesn't take much effort to soften the impact with plain fare.

If you like the idea of dressing in the most currently popular fashions and colors, set aside a little time to read about what colors complement each other, what styles of coats, dresses, jackets, jeans, sweaters and ties are "in." Looking stylish sometimes takes extra effort—but if you enjoy it, it's worth it.

Working Clothes

What clothes you should wear at your part-time job is no problem if you work at McDonald's or for your father's company. At McDonald's they will give you a uniform, and chances are you can wear whatever you like at your father's place of business without being hassled. However, many firms and service companies that employ young men and women do have certain ideas about how their employees, either part-time or full-time workers, should dress. If the job involves serving the public such as in a restaurant or department store, you should plan to dress in neat, clean clothes. Dirty jeans and worn-out T-shirts won't be very welcome. Here are some tips to help you dress appropriately for a job interview or your first days on the job.

If you are going on a job interview, chances are you will want to make a good impression on the person who will be evaluating you. Young men should consider wearing a shirt, tie and good trousers—even if the interview is for a factory job or employment at a car wash. Remember, you will most likely be talking to a manager or someone in authority, and it's not unlikely that this person will be dressed neatly in a shirt and tie. Young women have a wider range of clothing to choose from. Wearing a shirt or blouse and skirt or slacks might be a reasonable approach.

The best ways to determine what is appropriate for you to wear to your job are:

Ask your new boss or manager.
Observe what other workers are wearing on the job.
Ask a fellow worker.

If you are getting your job interview through the aid of a friend, ask him or her what you should wear to the job interview.

Provocative, suggestive or bizarre clothes aren't looked upon too favorably at most places of employment. Dressing in a disco outfit for a new job at the local drugstore won't win you instant acceptance. And dressing like Sid Vicious or Mick Jagger won't earn you fast advancement if you've gotten a job at a local hospital or nursing home.

Informal Dress

Informal dress suggests a range of clothes not generally worn at formal and semiformal events. Informal dress, however, does not mean you can wear any old thing, or even school or work clothes. Informal dress is a general code that applies to the way you would dress for the following occasions:

dances
luncheon parties/brunches
informal dinner parties
church or synagogue services
other social events, such as school gatherings, some
restaurant dining, teas, showers

What the man wears   Sports jackets with open shirts
or turtlenecks are just fine, and shirts and ties are always
attractive. Designer jeans or good dress jeans and sweaters
are also appropriate. Informal dress does not usually include short-sleeve sports shirts, T-shirts or beat-up work
jeans. These are best saved for more freewheeling, any-
thing-goes occasions.

What the woman wears   Dresses, attractive slacks,
designer jeans and blouses or sweaters, a suit with skirt or
pants are all appropriate. No tattered jeans or old T-shirts,
please. And do consider the colors and fit. Matching or
complementary accessories and shoes will always add to
your overall appearance.

Semiformal Dress

Many functions that are not as fancy as a tuxedo-and-gown
affair still require special concern about what you wear.
These include:

graduations
weddings (as a guest)
religious ceremonies

dinner parties
funerals and wakes
fancy restaurant dining

Although the dress code for these events is less rigid, conservative common sense and appropriateness should be your guide. A T-shirt and jeans don't fit in well at a sit-down dinner for twelve.

What the man wears Sport coat, shirt, and tie, or a suit, shirt, and tie with conservative trousers are generally called for on these occasions. For weddings, funerals, wakes, and certain religious ceremonies, a dark, solid colored suit (navy blue, dark gray) and conservative tie and shirt is the appropriate attire. These rules aren't hard and fast—but the "Sunday best" approach should be kept in mind. For some occasions, a turtleneck sweater may be worn instead of a shirt, and tie or modified western dress, instead of a suit. When in doubt, be conservative out of respect for the people and their special feelings for a special day: Wear a shirt, tie, and sport coat or suit.

What the woman wears There is a wide range of possibilities for women, particularly for girls and young women. Semiformal dress for women traditionally has been the cocktail dress (street-length but dressy), the afternoon dress (street-length, a less dressy fabric such as wool), or a suit with a dressy blouse. Now a woman may wear becoming evening pajamas to a dinner party (not for more serious occasions, however) or a pants suit to a graduation (not, hopefully, to a funeral or religious ceremony). Tact and respect for the occasion will dictate correct attire. If in doubt, ask your hostess what she and the others are wearing. In cold or rainy weather, choose your outerwear with some care. Try to avoid wearing a coat whose colors or style are inappropriate or clash with your outfit—especially at an occasion like a church service, where you will probably keep your outerwear with you.

Formal Dress

Some rare occasions call for clothes that are very different from what we generally wear. Such special events might be:

> proms and dances
> weddings (member of the wedding party)
> charity ball
> debutante or coming-out party
> formal dinner party

What the man wears   In most instances, these occasions call for *black tie* dinner clothes (sometimes called tuxedos). The invitation will always say so, usually on the bottom left of the card. Traditional dinner clothes consist of black bow tie, a formal dinner jacket, and formal trousers. The lapels of the dinner jacket and the stripe of the trouser leg are faced with satin. Although black is the most popular color, midnight blue is acceptable. White linen jackets may be worn in summer and, for less formal parties, plaid or madras dinner jackets for hot weather. A formal white shirt with stud buttons, a waistcoat or a cummerbund, black socks, and black shoes are the accessories for dinner clothes.

White tie events are a rarity now. The invitation will state *white tie,* and this calls for a black tailcoat and trousers, high wing collar, white bow tie, starched shirt, white waistcoat and gloves. Unless you have your eye on the diplomatic corps, you will probably never find yourself in this formal wear. There may be one kind of occasion, however, in which you will wear a cutaway coat and striped trousers or black cutaway coat and white tie, and this is if you are getting married or if you are a member of a wedding party. Because these occasions in any man's life are so few, most communities have rental outlets where the appropriate dress wear can be rented overnight. They provide the entire outfit, including the cuff links, studs, gloves, socks, cummerbund—all the details, even the black shoes. Beware, however, of the somewhat gaudy souped-up tuxedos that may be offered as rental suits. Canary yellow tuxedos with floral piping or electric blue outfits with silver piping are a bit too powerful for most events. Where possible, your outerwear should be conservative and long— such as a raincoat, topcoat or overcoat. Bomber-type jackets or plaid parkas don't fit well with formal dress.

What the woman wears   There is a greater range of choice for women in dressing for formal dances or parties. Full-length evening or dinner dresses, very dressy (the word *dressy* does *not* mean fancy) cocktail dresses of just-below-the-knee length may be worn in any fashionable evening color. Heels, stockings and evening bags are necessary accessories. Pants suits are *not* being worn at formal weddings, debutante balls, or proms yet!

Give some attention to your outerwear. Full-length mink certainly isn't necessary, but any color or style that clashes strongly with your dress is best avoided. A simple, conservative shawl or coat is fine. And since you will probably be checking your outerwear as you enter, don't be too concerned about it.

A final word: Most formal events are to be enjoyed. Try not to wear clothes that don't fit or that need constant adjusting. Comfort, not misery, is the goal.

Chapter 9 ★ Special Events, Special Behavior

As long as you are living on this planet, there will be special events you will have to attend. At some of these occasions, you may be the star attraction—for instance, at your own graduation or wedding. At others, you will be a guest or a visitor—for instance, at someone else's graduation or wedding (shower, christening, bar mitzvah). Each of these special events has some accepted procedures, rituals, or courtesies that must be observed. For example, turning up at a funeral service in a hot pink jump suit or at a wedding ceremony in black veil and dress can be jarring and even disruptive.

As always, the wisest thing to do is to seek advice when you are uncertain about the correct dress and behavior. Ask someone close to the source—the bride's mother, the father of the graduating person, a close friend of the bereaved family. A tactful inquiry can save you from feeling uncomfortable.

This chapter focuses on what to do, how to dress, and how to respond to those occasions and events where you will be a guest or general participant. If you need more detailed guidance about these occasions, you can find books that cover them in every aspect.

Weddings and Wedding Receptions

Here are a few guidelines to make being a wedding guest easier.

When you receive an invitation, be sure to respond promptly. Those planning the occasion need to know how many will attend. Often there is an R.S.V.P. card that makes it easy to respond to the invitation.

Most invitations are for both the wedding ceremony and the reception that follows. However, not everyone can afford a big wedding reception, and sometimes the invitation may only be for the church ceremony or synagogue. Check your invitation carefully.

It is considered poor manners to ask the prospective bride or groom for an invitation to the reception.

What to wear to the wedding (unless you are in the wedding party) is described on pages 53–55—under Semiformal Dress. Basically, women wear cocktail dresses, and men wear suits or sport coats with shirts and ties.

Be sure to arrive and get seated before the ceremony begins. The general seating rules are: Family and friends of the bride are seated on the left side of the church or synagogue, and family and friends of the groom are on the right.

The tradition with respect to the wedding gifts is as follows:

> —If you are invited to both parts of the marriage celebration (ceremony and reception), you are obliged to give a gift to the couple. It is appropriate to send wedding gifts to the home of either the bride or the groom. Many brides have registered their pattern preferences at local stores. Those interested may phone the bride's family for the names of the stores.
>
> —If you are only invited to the religious ceremony or merely receive an after-the-wedding announcement, you are under no obligation to send a gift. It's up to you.

Engagement Parties and Wedding Showers

The basic rule for each of these events involves gift giving. At an engagement party, no gift need be brought because the engagement is to be announced at the party. Go and enjoy it. Among friends, an engagement present may be sent later on.

If you are invited to a wedding shower, you are expected to bring a moderately priced gift. If the shower has no special theme, a household item is always a welcome gift. These days men are now being invited to what was once an entirely female affair, so both must be prepared to invest in some kitchen utensils or a dish towel or two.

Remember, a shower gift is not a substitute for a wedding gift. If you are also invited to the wedding, you'll have to send another present later on.

Christenings

Most christenings are small affairs held at the church or home and followed by a simple party. Only the godparents are required to bring a gift for the newborn. Often this gift is something personal, such as a monogrammed spoon, hairbrush, or cup for the baby. Others often bring a trifle for the baby or flowers for the parents, but this isn't necessary.

Wakes, Funerals and Shiva

A wake affords people an opportunity to pay their last respects to the deceased and to visit with the bereaved. When you and your family or friends attend a wake, the simple procedure is:

Walk up to the casket for a moment of silence or prayer.

Visit with the bereaved family, perhaps expressing your feelings with such words as: "I'm very sorry."

If you are a stranger or distant relative/friend, it helps if you tell the bereaved family who you are or how you knew the deceased.

If possible, make an effort to attend the funeral services or wake or to visit a family sitting shiva. Your presence will be noted and appreciated. Flowers, a mass card and a sympathy note are traditional ways of expressing sorrow and respect. Candy or fruit are customarily brought to a family sitting shiva.

Graduations

The general guidelines about attending graduations are:

Go if you can—graduations are important celebrations of a lot of years of work and achievement. If you can't go, call or write to refuse right away. Seats are often limited.

Graduation gifts are optional and depend on your relationship to the person who's graduating. A note or card is always welcome.

At the reception following the ceremony, try not to monopolize the graduate's time and attention. It is a time of partying for many, and the graduates want to celebrate with each other.

First Communion or Confirmation, Bar Mitzvahs, Bas Mitzvahs

These events are religious as well as joyous occasions. They are celebrations for the young. If you are invited to attend, keep in mind that the specific ceremonies are generally conducted in a house of worship, and dress accordingly. Families of celebrants give gifts; you may either bring a gift or simply send a card.

Debutante Balls

Chances are you will never attend a debutante ball either as a participant or as an escort. Although this type of event has very limited appeal, it is still part of the American social scene, and it won't hurt you to know about it.

Debutante balls or coming-out parties provide a public opportunity for a family to introduce their daughter (usually between the ages of sixteen and eighteen) to the community. Traditionally, it is a formal dress affair. The young women are generally introduced in a group ceremony. Sometimes there are private parties that take place before or after the debutante ball.

If you are invited as a male escort, you will most likely be expected to appear in a tuxedo, and you will be one of two escorts traditionally required for the young lady being introduced. Typically, you will be told about the appropriate dress code in advance. There may even be a rehearsal or two.

Part THREE ★
IT'S PARTY TIME!

Chapter 10 ★ Giving a Party

The purpose of most parties, whether simple get-togethers or big budget productions like a New Year's Eve celebration, is to create a pleasant, entertaining atmosphere for your friends to enjoy. It doesn't hurt your popularity either, and it can be a great way to get to know someone you might be interested in. If you are just beginning to do some home entertaining, it's probably best to start with a simple party—just inviting a small group of friends, maybe all of the same sex, for openers. Unless you are super efficient and competent, don't start out by inviting one half of the freshman class or the entire football team. Giving a party should be enjoyable for you too, and it most likely will be enjoyable if you keep in mind the following suggestions and hints.

What's Involved

If you are planning to invite more than a handful of friends, it's a good idea to sit down (well in advance) and get clear about your party plans and the preparations you have to make. Go over everything with your parents to be sure you have family approval and cooperation. Here's a checklist that you might want to use.

What kind of party do I want—informal get-together, birthday party, graduation party or pool/barbecue party?

Who and how many people shall I invite—just close friends, friends of friends, schoolmates, relatives, neighbors, or the entire school?

What kind of entertainment will I have—stereo music and dancing, television (watching the Super Bowl, World Series, Olympics), home movies, swimming or other sport, or games?

When will the party be held—at night, during the day, on a weekend or a holiday?

What will be served to the guests—just soft drinks; beer and wine (if you are old enough and your parents approve) and snacks; a sandwich and/or salad meal; hot food; special punch?

How much money will the party cost—for refreshments, paper plates, cups, party favors, etc.?

Will adults be present to supervise?

Who will help prepare for the party (if it is a big one)?

Type of Party

There are all kinds of parties, and some are easier to give than others. Probably the most popular is a simple get-together which you can have at any hour, at any time, on any day. Soft drinks, potato chips, pastries or other snacks are the usual fare. This event doesn't take much preplanning, and the budget requirements are low. Everything is casual and informal.

If you want to celebrate a special occasion or create a special occasion, you can arrange something on a bigger scale—inviting ten or fifteen friends and perhaps serving sandwiches, cold cuts, pastry or even a hot buffet meal. Parties of this nature usually take some advance planning, invitations, a budget and the help of friends or parents. How you put together your party will depend on how formal you wish to be, whether there is a special theme involved (Halloween, New Year's Eve, etc.), how many people you want to invite, and how long the affair will last. It's pretty much up to you.

There are also parties that may be joint ventures or co-sponsored, such as when some friends get together and hold a surprise birthday party, going-away party or wedding shower. And finally, there are the more organized parties given by a class club, a church youth group or a sports club. These too require planning and cooperative effort.

Remember: Anyone can give a party, and the party doesn't have to be perfect—just fun.

Party Occasions

You don't ever need a special reason or occasion to give a party, but if you are searching about for a theme, you might consider the following.

birthday/sweet sixteen
New Year's Eve
graduation
going away/military enlistment
Christmas
Easter
Fourth of July
Election Eve
fall harvest
Halloween
Valentine's Day
Groundhog Day
new pool/swim
April Fools'
after the school prom
Thanksgiving
football game

If none of those seem to fit or if they aren't creative enough for you, it's perfectly all right to concoct your own party occasion such as "Good-bye cast on my leg."

The Entertainment

One thing you already know about parties is that for the most part, people entertain themselves. However, it doesn't hurt to consider some additional entertainment to get things warmed up or to provide an easy way for people to approach each other.

Music and dancing are probably the most popular forms of entertainment devised by modern man. Music generally helps set a mood. It should be kept at a volume that permits your guests to talk without shouting (and your neighbors to sleep). Try to be sensitive to different musical tastes. If your music library is limited, you might ask some friends to bring a few albums or tapes.

Theme parties often have their own traditional forms of entertainment, bobbing for apples for example, at Halloween or an egg hunt at Easter. An April Fool's party can include all kinds of pranks, and pool parties have their own natural watery entertainment.

The television set can be the focal point of some parties—Super Bowl, election night, Kentucky Derby, World Series. Be sure you have room enough for everyone to comfortably view the event. Borrow a second set if you think it will help.

Electronic games have become a new source of entertainment.

Picture slides of vacations are now being supplanted by home movies and video-recorded movies.

However you schedule your entertainment, do leave some time for simple unstructured partying. Most parties function very well on three major ingredients:

good company
good food
good music

Whom To Invite

The primary rule is that you invite the people you want to invite unless there are strong reasons not to. You might, for example, wisely decide not to invite someone because of a recent romantic breakup or because the person doesn't get along with one of your friends.

If you are planning a fairly large party, it will help if you make up a list in two parts:

> definitely want to invite
> will consider inviting

You might find yourself adding to one list or deleting from the secondary list as you make your preparations for the party.

Some additional guidelines you might consider are:

> Some people tend to be a bit shy and reserved at parties, so it helps to invite a few life-of-the-party types to loosen everyone up and get things moving.

> Try not to invite so many people that the result is a badly overcrowded party. Too many people usually leads to food and drink shortages, spills, stains or sometimes damaged furniture (three people in a chair).

> If you are planning a mixed party, try to balance the quota of men and women. One of the attractions of a party is the presence of the opposite sex. A party consisting of sixteen men and four women can get pretty competitive, and the few women can become exhausted from dancing.

The Invitations

There are three ways to invite people to your party.

In-person invitations are the most direct and provide you with an immediate answer. When extending the personal invitation, it is best to do it in private so that others (whom you don't intend to invite) won't overhear and feel slighted. There is, of course, the chance that people can forget the date of a verbal invitation. So do remind those you have invited of the date of your party beforehand.

Telephone invitations are an immediate and private way to extend an invitation—and pencil and pad are more likely to be available to note the date.

Written invitations are the most formal means of inviting your guests to your party. You can buy printed invitations with blanks for time and date, dress and address at local stationery or department stores. If you are creative, you can make them yourself with your own designs.

R.S.V.P. is written on your invitation when you want to make sure of a response, either an acceptance or a regret. You can write R.S.V.P. at the bottom of the invitation.

R.S.V.P.—address (for a written response)
R.S.V.P.—telephone number (for a verbal response)

Sometimes an R.S.V.P. is requested only if the invitee does not plan to attend. The invitation should so specify: *R.S.V.P.—regrets only.*

Lead time or advance notice should be ten to fourteen days before the party. If it is a New Year's party, or dinner party, three to four weeks is the more appropriate advance notice.

Greeting Your Guests—Getting Started

When your guests begin to arrive, your first job will be to make them comfortable. Greet them at the door. When possible, introduce them to any strangers. Show the guests where to put their coats and perhaps point to the refreshments and drinks.

Sometimes getting the conversation started may take a bit of effort. Breaking the ice doesn't require any great wisdom—merely a few facts or pieces of information that can be used to get a person talking.

> EXAMPLES:

> "Debby, I heard that you spent Christmas vacation mountain climbing in New Mexico. What was it like?"

> "Skip, someone said you were starting your own rock group. Who is in it?"

> "Did anyone see the basketball game Friday night? What did you think of it?"

Something To Eat and Drink

What you serve your guests will depend on a number of factors, including the size of the crowd, your budget and the nature of the party. You can make it as simple as soft drinks and snacks or as elaborate as full buffet dining with salad, entrée and dessert. As mentioned earlier, it's probably wise to start your party giving on a small scale till you feel comfortable and confident in your talent for throwing a large and/or elaborate party. For some, the dividing line between a simple party and something special is the kind of food to be served. Hot food, even just hot dogs or hamburgers (or a few warm snacks such as cheese puffs), requires much more effort and planning.

Food service can range from the ridiculous to the sublime. Pick the one that feels comfortable and affordable to you. Here is a range to consider.

chips and dips
cheese and nuts
fruits
cut-up vegetables and dip
cold cuts (make your own sandwich)
sandwiches (full or squares)
salad (vegetable or fruit)
salad dishes—potato salad, macaroni salad
hamburgers, hot dogs, pizza slices
hot entrée (keep it simple)
ice cream, cake, pastries

If you plan to offer hot food, it's probably easiest if you set up a buffet table or sideboard where the food, plates, utensils and napkins can all be assembled together. Unless you want to be very formal, most party crowds do nicely with paper plates (heavy-duty ones for hot food) and paper or plastic cups. Check in advance to be sure that you have enough serving bowls and trays for the food.

A few final tips if you are having a sizable party with food are:

Enlist one or two friends or parents to help you with the preparation and serving.

Always order more food and drink than you think you will need.

Make a list of your needs and the costs well in advance.

Don't wait till the last minute to pick up the supplies.

Be sure you have enough ice—especially for summer parties.

If the party is being held outdoors, be sure there are enough tables for serving and receptacles for used plates, garbage, etc. If it is summer, use some pest spray before the party—mosquitoes love to crash parties.

The Party's Over.

When the party is over, what's left are fond memories and the task of cleaning up. With disposable plates and cups, your work is less difficult. You can also lighten the load if you:

Try to clean up some of the debris while the party is in progress.

Enlist the aid of one or two friends to help you at the end of the party. Some of the best fun can be comparing notes about your party experiences while cleaning up.

Chapter 11 ★ Going to Parties, Houseguesting

Partygoing

There are many ways to make your partygoing more relaxed, more fun, more interesting. Even before you leave your home, there's a bit of preparation that calls for consideration.

Be sure to inform your parents about the where, when, and with whom of your partygoing, and what time you expect to be home. It's even nicer to leave a telephone number where you can be reached in case of emergency. Remember, your parents are really concerned about your well-being.

If you are uncertain about what to wear, by all means

call your host or a friend, and ask what other people will be wearing. Don't feel awkward about it, people do it all the time.

If you want to bring a friend who hasn't been invited, it is good manners to call in advance and ask permission. Although it may be acceptable to bring an uninvited friend, it is downright inconsiderate to arrive with a tribe. Most parties have a budget, and a whole lot of unexpected guests can severely strain the food and supply lines as well as lead to overcrowding and resentment.

Once you arrive at the party, some simple courtesies can make the party more enjoyable for you and others. These include:

Introduce your date to the others, and help to introduce strangers. Often people are a bit uncomfortable or shy at parties; your kindness and ice-breaking actions can only increase everyone's pleasure.

When you can, make an effort to help the host with little chores such as carrying food, helping with drinks, serving snacks or emptying ashtrays and wastebaskets. Usually, the host is under pressure greeting people, fielding telephone calls, preparing the food or snacks and resupplying drinks. Your efforts will always be appreciated.

Think twice before you make any decision about bringing pot or hard liquor to a party. Drugs won't necessarily liven up the party or the people. Most parties do just fine without any mood changers.

If you do bring alcohol or pot, don't press anyone to use it.

Be sure to thank your host at the end of the party. Don't just slip out without a farewell.

If you are one of the last to leave, offer to help with the cleanup. When you have a party, you will welcome such an offer. Try to leave when the party is supposed to end.

Weekend Guesting

Being a weekend guest at a friend's or relative's home can be a pleasant adventure. Usually, as a guest, you get fussed over and treated in a somewhat special way. Try not to let all this good living go to your head. Offer to help and be a thoughtful guest. Sure it's nice to be waited on and pampered, but don't go looking for it or expecting it all the time.

You are much more likely to be invited back again and again if you keep in mind the following suggestions:

If you are uncertain about what clothes to pack, ask about what is planned (swimming, skiing, boating, a party or just lazing around, etc.), so that you can bring the right clothes.

Observe the daily routine with respect to meals, sleeping hours, etc. If the family goes to bed early, go to bed too, even if you're not sleepy. If breakfast is served at eight thirty, ask to be awakened and don't straggle down at ten o'clock. Make it a point to adapt yourself to the family schedule.

Be on time for meals. It's impolite to keep others waiting or the cook struggling to keep the food warm.

When in doubt about schedules, be sure to ask. Crossed signals are confusing and embarrassing.

Try to pitch in and help with the basic chores such as preparing sandwiches, setting and clearing the table and chopping or preparing things in the kitchen. Also, keep your bedroom (or your part of it) neat. This includes making your own bed. And don't forget to clean up the bathroom after using it. Attention to the little things is always appreciated.

Be cooperative about planned activities. If there's a picnic and you don't like ants, bugs, green grass or sunshine, try to be adaptable. If a fishing trip is planned and you hate to fish, try to be agreeable. If you are allergic to insect bites or get violently seasick, simply extend your apologies and give your reasons. No host or hostess wants to cause you discomfort.

If you have special needs, such as attending church, you should bring them up when you first arrive. That way plans can be worked out in advance. Don't be bashful or hesitant. It's also helpful to talk to your host or hostess about departure plans so that there are no mix-ups on either side.

If you borrow anything during your stay—a sweater, razor, brush, book, etc.—be sure to return it before you leave. And when you get ready to depart, make a second check around your room to be sure that you aren't leaving any of your belongings.

Don't extend your stay unless a delay in departure has been agreed to in advance or fairly early in your visit. If you are visiting with a friend/relative at his or her parents' home or vacation house, be sure that any extension is approved by the parents. An extended visit could pose a problem if the adults have made other plans or are expecting other guests when you leave.

Writing a thank-you note within a few days of your return home is a simple, easy-to-do courtesy that should never be skipped.

Chapter 12 ★ Party Problems

Parties can and should be fun. However, even the best of parties can have a few problems.

Party Attendance

Most people worry about no one showing up. They think that a party is a test of their social popularity. Perhaps the best way to rid yourself of that nagging fear of no one showing up is to consider the following:

Most people want to go to parties. They enjoy them.

People tend to arrive late at parties. For some reason, it's not popular to be the first to arrive.

You usually go to the parties you are invited to attend.

Will Your Guests Get Along With Each Other?

Generally, most guests are quite capable of doing their own socializing. However, a few simple courtesies and tactics can increase the party enjoyment.

Be sure to introduce your guests to each other. Don't just ignore your guests once they have arrived. In an introduction, try to include a descriptive comment to turn strangers into acquaintances.

EXAMPLES:

"John, this is Jack Kelly, the captain of our football team."

"Debbie, I'd like you to meet Laura. You both have something in common—tennis."

If it's too quiet at the beginning of your party, find the guest who is the life of the party, the showman or the chattiest girl, and pull them into a group with the quieter guests.

If one or two of your guests are wallflowers, give them a job, such as passing snacks and filling glasses.

If you notice close friends huddling together instead of mixing, try these simple tactics:

EXAMPLES:

"Sue, why don't you and Don come with me to the kitchen. There's another couple I'd like you to meet."

"Bob, come meet Nancy. She's just arrived, and you'll love her."

The Uninvited

The good party-giver usually stands close enough to the front door to greet each guest personally. Every once in a while, someone who hasn't been invited appears at the front door. Just about everyone has been faced with this problem at one time or another. And there are no clear-cut rules about how to respond. If someone or several people who are rowdy or obviously drunk arrive, the best approach might be to step outside with him, her, or them and say:

> "I'm sorry, but this is a special party, and you weren't invited."
> "This isn't an open house. I would appreciate it if you would leave."

If the party crashers slip by you or enter when you aren't looking, it's perfectly all right to corner them privately and ask them to leave. It's not a pleasant task, and you may not want to hurt their feelings. But then the crashers weren't particularly concerned about your feelings.

Naturally, you can, if you like, invite them in. But don't let yourself feel pressured. It's perfectly all right to stand your ground and ask crashers to go. In some instances, the uninvited may appear clean and neat and presentable. If you know them by name, and it is a good-sized party, you can welcome them without a fuss and invite them in. However, if the crashers are total strangers, neat, clean or not, it's a good idea to avoid trouble and not invite them in.

If they claim to know or to have been invited by one of your guests, you might ask the person named to come and deal with the crashers. Just keep in mind that each situation is different, and try to use your own best judgment and a little tact.

If the Party Gets Rough

Unfortunately, there are occasions when the party giver may really be put to the test. If a shouting match, argument, or brawl begins at your party, try these simple home remedies.

Separate the feuding parties as quickly as possible. If possible, get them into different rooms. If the contestants are too big or wild for you to handle, enlist the aid of whoever can handle them.

If pot and/or alcohol are being liberally or openly passed around and you're not keen about it, ask the users to respect your wishes and wait until the end of the party to indulge.

If the police appear, called by a neighbor, be sure to cooperate politely. They are called to many party disturbances; all they want is reasonable consideration and respect. If you need police help with crashers or brawling guests, don't be afraid to ask for it. It's your party: You and your guests have the right to enjoy it.

Chaperones

If you want adult help, don't hesitate to ask. Most parents are willing to take a quiet and useful part in the party. Your friends may feel a bit awkward in your parents' presence for a few minutes, but don't worry. They will loosen up soon enough and so will your parents.

If you are told that you must have chaperones, accept the decision gracefully. Their presence can be a blessing in disguise in many ways. Don't forget to introduce them to the guests, particularly those guests who might prove troublesome.

Good parent-chaperones understand about keeping a low profile. They don't have to be in the same room as the party—just in the same house.

Will I Run Out?

That problem everybody worries over—running out of food or drinks—generally takes care of itself. Most people share as the food thins out or are good sports if they arrive too late to get much to eat. If inaccurate planning—or too many guests—leave you a bit short, you can either send or go out for more, or just let the party take its course without refreshments.

People don't care that much how much food there is. At least most people don't. Usually they come to a party to be with each other and with you. And usually they have a fine time.

Being Entertained

There may be an instance when you are at a party given by someone else, and trouble descends on you. Some problems you might have to contend with are:

The disappearing date Some dates may be elusive and difficult to track down at a party. That's not as unusual as you may think. However, if your date vanishes, you will have to make some decisions.

Decide to enjoy the party on your own, and make arrangements to go home with another couple or unattached person.

Make a thorough effort to locate the person, and then make the necessary plans to go home alone.

Give your date the benefit of the doubt, assume she or he will turn up later, and don't worry yet about leaving the party.

The date who takes a trip If your date chooses to get carried away by hard liquor or pot or other drugs at a party, his or her behavior could ruin your good time and that of others. Here are a few options you might consider if you decide to take action.

You can grin and bear it, preferring not to make waves. Just be polite, keep your distance, and start planning alternative transportation home.

Tell the person how you feel about his or her behavior, and request that he or she consider your feelings.

If your date is clearly more interested in getting high than in being with you, and you don't feel like being a bystander, say you would like to leave. Your date can accompany you or not. Your actions may not be popular. But then your date's actions are clearly rude and inconsiderate.

Liquor, drugs and driving can be a lethal combination. If your partner, or the person planning to drive you home, can't navigate well, don't take a chance. Find another way to get home. You can avoid becoming a highway statistic or disfigured for life—you just have to say, "No thanks. I'll ride with someone else."

The forward pass Both men and women have to be prepared for that aggressive and sometimes rudely persistent forward pass. Whether you are alone or with someone, an unwelcome hustle needs to be dealt with directly. If you fancy the forward pass, then good luck! If you aren't pleased, it is best to be direct and tactful.

EXAMPLES:

"No, thank you." (And walk away!)

"Thanks, but I'm seeing someone." (Be firm!)

"Really, I'm not in the mood." (Don't sound as if you're flirting.)

Actually, the words used are less important than the tone. If you *mean* no, *sound* no.

Part FOUR ★
SMALL TALK

Chapter 13 ★ Please, May I, Thank You, I'm Sorry

When you were young, you probably were subjected to a continuous running lesson in "early manners." Mixed with your ABC's were those wonderful phrases:

"Say *please.*"
"Don't forget to say *thank you.*"
"When you do something like that, say *I'm sorry.*"

It was all part of your early training, and now it's part of your daily chatter and small talk—or it should be. Only a few words are involved, short words, easy words to get your mouth around. No one pays too much attention to these words when you say them. But you can bet that their absence is noticed. ("You know who George is—he's the one who never calls to say *thank you* for the party." "How

87

can you forget Sally? She's the one who can't get *I'm sorry* past her teeth.'')

If It Pleases You

There are literally hundreds of situations when the words *please may I* can bring a quicker, warmer, more friendly response. Some of the more notable occasions center around mealtimes, parties and entertaining, borrowing and seeking assistance or directions. Here are a few occasions to show that manners matter to you.

Mealtimes   If the food you want is out of your reach or not in sight, it really is easy to enlist the aid of others with a simple, ''Please may I have the chicken?'' It sure beats the reach-and-grab school of dining. You can vary this with, ''Please pass the cream.'' ''May I please have some more corn?'' ''May I please be excused?'' ''Would you please bring our check?'' People are fed far more often in this world because of their good, appreciative manners than for their fascinating conversation.

Parties and entertaining   One of the toughest lines to deliver, if you're giving a party, is ''Please keep the noise down—our neighbors still like us.'' Or ''Thanks for using the coasters; the tabletops don't hold up too well.'' Or ''May I give you a plate and napkin to put under your sandwich?'' Or ''I'm really so sorry, but it's one o'clock in the morning and I've got to be at the dentist's at eight.'' These, however, are far more polite, more easily swallowed by guests than, "Shut up" or "My, aren't you sloppy!" or "For god's sake, get out of here, I'm exhausted."

Other lines that smooth out party discomfort, or the discomfort of any gathering, are: "May I join you?" "Won't you please join us?" "Please let me help you with . . ." "I'm so sorry, but I've forgotten your name." "Thank you for a lovely evening." As opposed to these, consider the gracelessness of: "Push over." "Comover here." "Lemme do it." "Geez, who're you?" Or "Gimme an invite back, huh?"

Manners do add warmth to groups of people, from parties to subways. Too often, they come as a pleasant surprise, instead of as a matter of course.

Borrowing It's not unusual for people to get sensitive or cranky when one of their possessions is borrowed without notice. A major test of your manners is your willingness to ask before you borrow.

"May I please borrow your recorder?"

"I would appreciate it if you would lend me your car for tonight." (Smile as you say this in your friendliest manner.)

"I'm sorry to ask again, Brenda, but my hair dryer is still out of commission."

Your family may be even more appreciative of your good manners than people you seldom see. And since they're the ones you probably borrow most from, you may get far better results by remembering this courtesy. And don't forget to return the borrowed item promptly and in good condition. Don't wait till you get badgered about it.

Seeking assistance and directions People forget that they are not automatically entitled to the time, help, and consideration of everyone around them. Do be verbally gracious and thankful when you ask someone for advice or directions about how to get somewhere or to do something. Next time you need something from someone, consider starting the conversation with one of these attention-getting statements:

"Would you please held me with . . . ?"

"Thank you for stopping. Can you please tell me how to get to the airport?"

"I'm sorry to bother you, but would you mind holding my place in line?"

The Fine Art of Saying Thank You

Thank you is something people really remember when you forget to say it. How often have you heard someone criticize, "And he/she didn't even say thank you—after all I did." There are no special rules about how often to say thank you, but there are a few times and occasions when it's really better not to forget to.

When people extend a simple courtesy to you such as opening a door, holding a chair, moving aside in public places to make room or giving you a seat on a bus, do acknowledge such gestures with a smile and your thanks.

When you are paid a compliment or praised for anything from your singing to your pitching to your new dress, a thank-you is far more appropriate than "Oh, yeah?'' ''Nah, I was terrible.'' Or ''You mean this old thing?''

When you've had an enjoyable evening with someone (having nothing to do with who paid, whose house you were at, how good the movie was), the someone will probably brighten up if you say ''Thanks so much, I've had a marvelous time with you.''

When you've been to a party, to dinner at someone's home, even just over for a cup of coffee, a thank-you is essential. The more elaborate the entertainment, the more special the thank-you ought to be. An immediate verbal thank-you at the door is enough for a cup of coffee; for dinner, a thank-you at the door and a phone call the next day are in order; for a more elaborate party, a thank-you at the door, and either a phone call the next day or a note of thanks are considered good form.

Other occasions when a special thank-you is warranted include:

When you are served anything, from dinner in a restaurant to gas at a gas station to help in a store—people who wait on people deserve a thank-you as well as your business.

When you receive a present—always—whether you like them or not!

Rides home, favors of any kind, a thoughtful phone call, a book lent to you.

Thanks needn't be gushy or overdone. Just the two words said with feeling will do fine for most circumstances.

I'm So Sorry, Excuse Me

Accidents happen all the time. They are a natural part of being out and about. And short of running over someone with the family car, you are most likely going to be forgiven for the spills, breakages, collisions and mishaps of life—especially if the words immediately following the incident are "I'm so sorry," or "Please excuse me."

Some of the more common occurrences when an apology can soothe a set of ruffled feathers are:

Bumping or jostling someone, especially when you're in a hurry. Don't just toss the apology over your shoulder as you speed on. Stop to see if the other person is all right.

Interrupting a conversation—whether you have an urgent need or not—merits an "I'm sorry to interrupt" or a "Please excuse me."

Lateness, whether in person or for an uncompleted project, requires an apology.

If you spill something on someone, you apologize *and* help to clean up, or at least offer to. As with a collision, don't just walk away muttering an apology—become part of the solution.

Breaking a household object, denting a car, or damaging someone else's property in any way are examples where "I'm sorry" can be carried out not just on the verbal level but also on the level of action. You inform the owner of your responsibility, say you're sorry, and ask how you can help, fix, pay for, replace, or otherwise compensate for the damage.

Displaying a bad temper or reacting in such a way as

to embarrass those around you (for example, friends or relatives), generally should be followed with an apology as soon as you can get things under control again. When tempers fly and people get upset, "Sorry about that" can ease the tension and show that you have respect for other people's feelings.

Do remember that verbal apologies are for trivial matters. If you have just dented the family car for the fourth time, the words *I'm sorry* do not quite cover the situation! The more serious the matter, the more "I'm sorry" must become an action or a change in attitude rather than just a few words.

But we all spill on couches, drop dishes, lose tempers, and step on people's toes. "I'm sorry" covers a lot of that quite nicely.

Chapter 14 ★ Beginning and Ending Conversations

Anyone can learn how to carry on a conversation. Even if so far you're only at your best two hours after the party is over or the person you've gone out with has gone home, you, too, can learn how to be more verbally nimble with more than your mirror for company. It does, however, take a bit of people practice—being willing to engage friends, acquaintances, and strangers in conversation. Fortunately, you don't need great wit, superior intellect, or Woody Allen's sense of humor. A good conversation doesn't consist of a continuous flow of one-line jokes or a two-hour, nonstop monologue—it's got to do with really caring about what you and the other people have to say. Remember, strangers are only people you haven't had a chance to talk with yet. The best way to avoid the problem of what-do-I-do-now-that-I've-said-hello is to practice some new approaches. The hardest parts of most conversations are the beginning and the end of them.

It All Begins With Hello.

First impressions may be superficial, but they are the first thing we give. So what you say, after you say hello, is important. Here we go.

Prepare yourself in advance.   If a friend is about to introduce you to a stranger, you can ask your friend a few quick questions so that you will have some advance information as conversational ammunition. For example:

> Where does he live?
> What school/college does she attend?
> Where is she working?
> Does he play football?

Observe the person, how he or she dresses, looks, acts. Learn to spot some things that can be used in conversation.

> "Are those the new Nike Daybreak running shoes? How do they feel?"
> "Is that the new Rolling Stones release?"
> "Do you have trouble with your Walkman radio?"

The opening comment doesn't have to be profound. It can be objective, chatty, even intimate if you choose—a personal remark brings on a quick, cozy feeling between strangers, especially if it's a compliment.

EXAMPLES:

"I was admiring your jacket; it fits you so well."

"Do you know anything about the new disco—Roberto's?"

"I just love your hair."

"How do you keep in such great shape working at Baskin Robbins?"

Think about how you are.   It's quite natural for people to say to you "How are you?" So before greeting a person, think for a moment about what's been happening to you and be ready with some answers.

EXAMPLES:

"I'm going on vacation to Colorado next week, and I'm excited about it."

"I've been working nights, and I really miss my free time."

"I've just finished trying out for the basketball team, and I hope I make it."

Do remember when meeting people for the first time not to: insult them instantly; insult yourself as a form of humor; blow your own horn or theirs too much too fast. In other words, try for something in between being too shy and coming on too strong.

Talking It Up

Once you're into the conversation, try the following:

Ask questions, and look for areas where you have something in common.

Listen to what is said; it can spark some thought or another comment.

If you're having trouble, getting bored, or feeling stuck, bring others into the conversation to broaden the group.

Talk about what's going on around you—the music or the band, or if it's a party, the party and the people there.

Talk about yourself and your experiences; you really are interesting to others.

Then shut up and let others talk about themselves; they are just as interesting as you are.

If you suddenly hit one of those deadly silences, let it happen. It's not your responsibility to keep all conversation going. If it gets too painful, ask a question that will require a bit of a response. Like: "Just how did you train for those all-state trials?" "How did you like the new Dustin Hoffman movie, Super Bowl game, etc.?"

If all else fails you, talk about the weather.

All's Well That Ends Well.

You'd be surprised at how many people don't know how to end a conversation or part company with ease. Take a few days and observe carefully how awkward, rude, or out of sorts people get as they are ending a discussion with you. Some will probably mumble a last sentence, toss out a quick farewell, and scurry away abruptly. Others may look at their shoes, do a shuffle, fidget, then begin talking fast and furiously as they back away from you. If you catch yourself in this posture, try something else instead.

When you decide to move on, be direct and pleasant. Say, "I've got to be going now. It's been so nice talking

to you." Or "Good night. Hope to see you again soon."
Or "Take care of yourself. See you later."

Do shake hands, kiss, embrace, pat, or make whatever physical gesture seems appropriate.

You can end a telephone conversation with a verbal
hug and say, "It's been great talking to you; thanks for
calling."

Whether you've come to the end of a business conversation, a social chat, a phone call, a chance encounter, or
a lively party discussion, there's no need for a Shakespear-
ean Act V farewell scene. Keep it direct, and keep it simple.

Part FIVE ★ LETTER-PERFECT

Chapter 15 ★ Invitations, Acceptances, Regrets, Thank-you's, Greeting Cards

The telelephone and the automobile have done much to eliminate the need for the written word. You can talk to or be with anyone so quickly these days. However, some occasions still call for a letter, a card, or a note. What you say, the quality of the paper or card, and whether you understand the correct form can be important—so important that there are whole books dedicated to these matters. What this chapter does is present some of the basic forms of formal correspondence.

Invitations

Although formal engraved (printed) invitations are used for very special affairs, informal invitations are generally in order. If your event is a very formal one, you can find information about formal invitations in a book that covers these details.

Less formal invitations for events such as a graduation party, a sweet sixteen party, or a wedding shower do require the basic pieces of information:

> name of the host
> date of the event
> time of the event
> place of the event
> response instructions

These may be written on plain stationery or filled in on preprinted invitations. Be sure to send your invitations well in advance—three to four weeks. The following are some examples of informal invitations.

Dinner party

Mr. and Mrs. Robert Snow
request the pleasure of your company
at a dinner
on Saturday, the tenth of April
at eight o'clock
200 Maple Street

R.S.V.P.

Sweet sixteen party

Mr. and Mrs. Robert Snow
request the pleasure of your company
at a sweet sixteen party
in honor of their daughter
Hannah
on Friday, June sixth
at eight thirty o'clock
200 Maple Street
R.S.V.P.

Dinner invitation (informal)

January 3

Dear Jill

Can you and Jack join me for dinner on Wednesday, January 21st, at 8 P.M.?

Nancy Granger

Cocktail and buffet party (semiformal)

You are invited by
Janet Wilson
for cocktails and buffet
on Friday, May fifth
at six thirty o'clock
92 Elm Street
R.S.V.P.

Christening party (semiformal)

> Sally and George Jones
> would like you to come and share
> in the christening ceremony and celebration
> of their daughter, Kathleen
> on Sunday, March tenth
> at four o'clock
> 957 Park Avenue
> R.S.V.P.

Acceptances and Regrets

It seems that the telephone has clearly replaced all but the most formal replies to invitations. However, if you decide to make a handwritten reply, the primary guidelines are:

If you received a formal invitation, it is customary to reply *exactly* in kind.

> *Lois Lane*
> *accepts with pleasure*
> *the kind invitation of*
> *Mr. and Mrs. John Harkins*
> *to the marriage of their daughter*
> *Laura May*
> *to*
> *Mr. George Harrison*
> *on Friday, the tenth of July*
> *etc.* (the whole thing!)

If the invitation is semiformal or informal, you may reply in a warmer, friendlier manner.

January 5

Dear Debby,

Thanks so much for your party invitation. It will be so much fun to see all of you. I can hardly wait.

My best,
Jill

On those occasions when you receive a formal invitation from a married couple, the accepted reply procedure is as follows. In a formal address, *his* name is first (Dear Mr. and Mrs. His Name); in an informal address, her name is first (Dear Her and Him). The only exception to the latter is if you're inviting the whole family, or writing to a lot of them. A string of names again requires his name first (Dear John, Jane, Little Felix, Baby Doll, and Doggie).

Always respond to an R.S.V.P. *promptly* by mail or telephone or in person. The R.S.V.P. request is most important to the person giving the party. If people fail to reply, the host or hostess won't know how many to expect or what preparations to make.

If you see the legend *R.S.V.P—regrets only,* you need *only* reply if you *cannot* attend.

Always address your reply to the person or persons who issued the invitation. If the event is to be held at a club or hotel, reply to the address and name listed with the R.S.V.P.

If you find that you will be unable to attend, your

letter of regret should be in the same style as the invitation. If you received a formal invitation, your reply must be equally formal.

Jane Snow
regrets that she is unable to accept
the kind invitation of
Mr. and Mrs. James Jones
for dinner
on Friday, the sixth of March
at eight o'clock

If the invitation was informal, your regrets might be:

February 25
Dear Jim,
I'm sorry that I won't be able to make it to your graduation party. Unfortunately, I will be on a hiking trip with my cousins. Have a wonderful party.
Yours,
Judy

Keep your acceptances or regrets short and pleasant, unless you feel compelled to write a special letter. If you find that you can attend the event after you have written your regrets, it's best to call and explain your new circumstances.

Thank-you Notes

Thank-you notes are always welcome and, in most cases, appropriate, after you've been entertained in a special manner (or been given special gifts, received special favors, or just happen to feel especially grateful). Be prompt in sending a thank-you note—sometimes warm feelings wear off. Even if you've verbally thanked someone for something special, a note is not only mannerly and impressive, it's something someone else can keep. You don't need special stationery or even special words.

The following are some typical situations for which a thank-you note might be in order: a Christmas, birthday, shower or graduation gift; a weekend or overnight visit as a houseguest; a formal dinner party; any dinner party; any party. In short, almost any time someone is nice to you in a special way, a note is a way to show your appreciation.

EXAMPLES OF THANK-YOU NOTES:

September 10

Dear Aunt Jean,

Thank you ever so much for the great pair of ski boots. They are a perfect birthday gift as I desperately needed a new pair for the coming season. It was so thoughtful of you.

With much love,
Betty

April 25

Dear Kathleen,

Thanks for a wonderful weekend. I always enjoy my visits to your great beach house. The weather and the sailing were just perfect.

My best,
Frank

Greeting Cards

Most greeting cards carry messages of good cheer, congratulations and friendship. They can be used on all sorts of occasions—even for announcing the arrival of a litter of new pups.

Choosing the right card for the right occasion is seldom a problem. Most people realize that you don't send a get-well card in response to a marriage announcement. The real problem is remembering the birth dates, anniversary dates, and so forth. Keeping an annual calendar of your own important dates helps.

A few things to remember about greeting cards are:

As beautiful as some of them are, they can seem impersonal, so do write a little something besides your name on them.

For the same reason (also because it's tacky), don't type your name or stamp it.

On Christmas and Channukah cards, write a few words of greeting, not just your name.

Holiday greeting cards may be sent to close as well as distant friends, but since a card may be more important to those who live at a distance, choose them first if a choice has to be made.

The human voice may be one of God's greatest miracles, but so is a well-written note. Be one of those who knows how to write one.

Chapter 16 ★ Business Letters

If you work in an office, the nature of the company you work for will provide you with the form and content of the business letters you write. They need only be clear and to the point.

Personal business letters written from your own home, such as a request to a company for merchandise, a request for a job interview or information, a letter about a faulty product, will be answered much more promptly and courteously if they seem to come from someone who is competent.

A few do's and a don't:

Do use a typewriter if you can, or at least write clearly in ink on personal or simple bond paper.

Don't use fancy stationery, colored Magic Markers, or pencil on scrap paper.

Do address the envelope clearly, and put a return address both on the envelope and on the letter itself.

Do keep a copy of all business correspondence in case of loss in the mail or questions.

The following examples may help.

A request for merchandise

35 East 75 Street
New York, NY 10021
October 20, 1982

Ms. Ann Durell
E.P. Dutton, Inc.
2 Park Avenue
New York, NY 10016

Dear Ms. Durell:

Please send by United Parcel the following books:

One copy of *Suspect* by Patricia Giff, $8.95
One copy of *The Frog People* by Dale Carlson, $8.95

These items are from your 1982 Spring catalog. Enclosed please find my check for $17.90.

Sincerely,

Joan Thompson

A request for a job interview

30 East 65 Street
New York, NY 10022
July 21, 1982

Mr. Charles Adams
116 East 63 Street
New York, NY 10021

Dear Mr. Adams:

In response to your advertisement in *The New York Times* on July 10, 1982, I wish to request an interview for the position of dog walker. I understand that you will need my services twice a day for the entire summer at $6.00 per hour. Please contact me to schedule an interview. My phone number is 855–1234.

Thank you for your consideration.

Sincerely yours,

Marie Harkins

A request for information

45 Melody Lane
Richmond, VA 23001
February 12, 1982

Manager
Washington Rock Concerts
895 K Street
Washington, DC 22123

Dear Sir:

I have been told that your firm is producing a rock concert in April that will feature the Rolling Stones. Please send me your promotion brochure or information about the concert dates, show schedules and advance ticket purchases. I have enclosed a stamped self-addressed return envelope for your convenience.

Very truly yours,

James Hicks

Inquiry about product replacement

145 Boardwalk Street
Columbus, OH 16432
October 1, 1982

Manager
Complaint Department
Inferior Manufacturing Company
Lowbottom, NV

Dear Sir:

One of my birthday gifts was your model P-5 portable radio-cassette player. Unfortunately, it does not work at all. I carefully followed your instruction booklet directions. There is no sound, and the cassette drive wheel doesn't work. I also purchased new batteries.

Kindly tell me how I can obtain a replacement unit. The stores in my area do not carry your products. Enclosed is a copy of my warranty card.

Very truly yours,

Carol Bennett

Neat letters have a way of communicating that their sender is adult, competent, solvent and responsible. They are usually answered promptly and positively.

Part SIX ★ EVERYDAY MANNERS

Chapter 17 ★ Friendly Visits

Simple hospitality and friendly visits don't require a lot of fuss or lavish preparations. Just a little planning ahead can help smooth the way whether it's a once-a-year visit to distant relatives or a visit to a hospitalized aunt.

Visiting Others at Home

Whether you are planning to visit someone today or two weeks from now, always consider these suggestions:

If they haven't already invited you, call *in advance.* Although a friend or relative may say "Drop in any time," the unspoken words are still "but call and give us a little advance notice." The distance to be traveled and the closeness of your relationship with the person you plan to visit should influence your approach to visiting.

If you are planning a once-a-year visit, do call or write in advance.

If you are planning an extended trek through towns or cities where you happen to have friends, be sure to let them know your plans in advance and wait for an invitation.

Impromptu visits (dropping in on very short notice), should, as a matter of courtesy, be kept short and sweet. Don't be surprised or disappointed if those you are visiting have made other plans or cannot spend too much time with you.

Hospital Visits

Before you visit, call the hospital and inquire about the visiting hours.

If the person you want to visit has been seriously ill or undergone surgery, contact close friends or relatives before visiting.

Do obey hospital rules not only about hours, but smoking, food and flowers, length of visit, whatever.

If the person you are visiting is sharing a room, be considerate of the other patients. Talk in low tones, and try not to wander about.

Try to avoid showing shock or too much concern about the condition of the patient. A sick person may be very sensitive and self-conscious about his or her condition.

A little something   Whether it's a hospital visit or a trip to visit a grandmother you seldom see, even if it's dinner with a close friend, it can be nice to bring along "a little something." A few flowers, fruit, homemade cookies are some of the "little somethings" that can be offered as a token of your appreciation. A gift will brighten up any visit, but it is never essential. Your good company and thoughtful ways are what count.

Others Visiting You

When you invite people to visit, you should prepare for them. If it is to be a short visit, you merely offer the hospitality of your home and something simple to drink and eat—just a soft drink, coffee, cookies will be enough, A meal invitation or an evening together requires more planning and probably clearance with your parents. An overnight guest will expect dinner and breakfast unless you have made other arrangements. However you work it out, remember that once you and/or your family have offered to play host, do it gracefully and with consideration for the comfort of your guests.

Unannounced Visitors

Among life's little surprises (they may or may not be pleasant surprises), are unannounced guests who arrive at your doorstep or call from around the corner.

Fortunately, there's a simple set of rules to cover this situation.

The first is that you are under no obligation to invite them in—your privacy comes first. But there is no need to be rude about it, since obviously they have been thinking nice thoughts about you, or they wouldn't be there in the first place. You can say, "I'm sorry, we're just going to bed." Or "We were dressing to go out." Or "We have other plans." You can add "How about tomorrow?" or just "Thanks so much for thinking of me."

If, however, you are pleased to hear from your friends, but you must keep the visit short because of homework or other demands, you can simply give them a drink and something to munch on. You are under no obligation to lodge them or feed them dinner. If they are expecting more, that's their problem.

If you are absolutely delighted to see them, you can all have fun putting together an impromptu day or evening.

Chapter 18 ★ Telephone Calls

They say telephone manners can reveal far too much about a person. The impression that you communicate over the telephone wires is truly a lasting one. Since the person at the other end of the line can't see you, most of the impressions they have of you are formed by how you present yourself when calling or answering the telephone. Grunts, mumbles, or snappish rude replies are just a few of the ways you can engrave a permanently bad impression. And since you have probably been on the receiving end of some ill-mannered callers, you know how disturbing such calls can be.

Somewhere in your history of telephone calls, you've had some pleasant experiences—a wonderful voice, a nice manner, an unexpected courtesy. Remember: People respond positively to warm, friendly voices (so do puppies and large, barking dogs) and negatively to harsh, abrupt, and unpleasant communications.

How To Answer a Telephone Call

Believe it or not, your local telephone company gives classroom instruction in good telephone manners. A lot of this instruction is aimed at workers who are in telephone contact with the general public. In the business world, good telephone manners are invaluable, and they surely can benefit you in your personal life. When answering a telephone, keep in mind the following pointers:

Start with a friendly, pleasant "Hello." Don't make a grunt or rude bark or snap "Yeah, waddya want?"

If the telephone call is for you, and you can't identify the voice, it's perfectly all right to interrupt and say, "Who is this?"

If the call isn't for you, you may say, "May I ask who's calling?"

If the family member isn't at home or is unavailable, ask if you can take a message. Be sure to write down the message, and to repeat out loud to the caller any telephone numbers you have been given.

Running interference for another household member who wants to pick and choose the calls he or she will receive is no fun. It can be embarrassing and complicated. It's best to tell the family member either to answer the calls herself/himself or to give advance instructions like "I don't want any calls after nine o'clock or while we're at dinner."

Don't leave someone waiting on the phone while you

take care of other activities such as changing the record or investigating a dog fight on your back lawn. If you want to leave the phone, suggest that either you or the caller call back. If you have to go to the barn to get the person wanted on the phone, mention this before leaving the caller just hanging there.

Callers trying to sell you something on the phone can be a headache. Be polite, listen to the preliminary introduction, then if you aren't interested, say so directly: "Thank you, but I'm not interested." Impatience and disinterest don't give you a license to growl and hang up. A policeman selling tickets to the Policemen's Ball might not forget your rudeness!

Crank calls are best handled by hanging up as soon as you discover what's happening. Don't play detective yourself. Call your local telephone company for assistance. Hang up immediately on an obscene phone call or right after you have blown a whistle into the phone. Never stay on the line out of curiosity, etc.

Manners for Telephoning Others

When you make a telephone call, naturally you want to reach a specific person quickly and pleasantly.

Identify yourself to the person who answers the phone. "Hello, this is Jim Mason, may I please speak to Marcia?" Don't lead off with "Marcia, please" or "Lemme speak to Marcia." If you recognize the voice of another family member, it is considered polite to say, "Good evening, Mrs. Brown, may I please speak to Clifford?" instead of just "Hello."

If the person you are calling isn't home, don't abruptly hang up. At least thank the person who answered the phone, and leave a message if you wish.

If you leave a message, thank the message taker. If the person doesn't offer to take a message, just ask.

Secretly listening in on an extension phone is not polite.

Avoid the "Guess who this is?" game; it isn't appealing to most people.

Try not to cross-examine the person answering the telephone if the person you want is not at home. Comments such as "Where is she?" "Who is he with?" "Where did she go?" are rude and invasive.

Try not to monopolize the telephone if it is the only one in the household. Remember: Even if others in your home do not wish to make a call, your continued use prevents any incoming calls.

Don't be long-winded in your telephone conversations. If you need a long chat, do ask first, "Have you got a few minutes?"

If the caller is talkative and could go on forever, it's perfectly acceptable to cut him or her short with "I'm sorry, I have to go now." "I hate to cut this short, but I have homework, got to help my mother, etc."

Should you mistakenly dial the wrong number, confirm that the number you reached is not the number you want, and offer your apology.

Operator Assistance

Telephone operators are professionals who are there to assist you. Although they are public servants, they aren't private serfs to be treated rudely and badgered. Chances are they can satisfy your telephone needs, and if for some reason they can't, don't be rude. Treat them as you would like to be treated if you had their job. Finally, don't request that the operator break in on a busy line unless there is a genuine emergency.

Chapter 19 ★ Gifts and Giving

For many young people, picking a gift can be a rough and confusing experience. Like most people, the gift giver wants his or her gift to be something really special, a gift that stands out and is long remembered. Short of a 4-karat diamond or an Alpha Romeo sports car, most gifts don't have such impact. Probably the most important thing to remember, when all the frantic searching and indecision are over, is that truly the thought counts more than the gift. You can avoid a certain obvious thoughtlessness, such as giving what is clearly a wrong-sized shirt. It's not too difficult to select a special-occasion present (graduation, shower, child's birthday). The pressure usually strikes when you're looking for a gift that conveys a particular sentiment or feeling.

Set yourself a budget. Whether it's five dollars or fifty dollars, have a price range in mind. You can eliminate a lot that way.

Start early. The more important (to you) the gift is, the more advance time you should give yourself. One way to avoid the last minute panicky feeling is to start your search when there is no immediate urgency.

Ask for advice. It's perfectly acceptable to ask friends, relatives, or shopkeepers for advice. Pick up catalogs to pore over so you don't have to make instant decisions. Wander through stores.

Be alert. Listen to hints from the person you want to buy a present for. Watch for clues. People often signal to others what they'd like to have, sometimes quite unconsciously. Some people don't, but some people do, like to be asked what they want for their birthday!

Make up a running list of ideas for presents for the recipient—and then check to make sure the person doesn't have them.

Make sure that the gift is appropriate. A Grateful Dead album won't be appreciated by an uncle who's a choir director any more than a heavily illustrated sex manual will be treasured as a gift from you to your parents. Humor is often fun, but most of the time it's best to play it straight.

For that special touch, gift wrap your present well. You'd be surprised at how attractive gift wrapping enhances the sentiment. Don't lessen the impact of your gift by sloppy wrapping. For about a dollar more, most stores will gift wrap for you.

Include a card. It's another chance to communicate your feelings.

If you've ordered a gift and it hasn't arrived in time, a special card explaining the situation should bail you out.

Chapter 20 ★ Lasting Impressions You Don't Want To Make

Here are a few not-so-wonderful impressions you should avoid making for everyone's sake.

Do not pop your bubble gum in rhythm with a string quartet presentation at your grandparents' golden wedding anniversary. And don't leave the worn-out gum stuck to the underside of the chair.

Do not demonstrate your interest in your houseguests by planting yourself in front of the television set and turning on a horror movie or, worse, women's wrestling matches.

Do not put your wet glass on a rare antique table at your friend's home.

Do not break into the movie line in front of some easily intimidated third graders.

Do not sneeze into your soup when you have a napkin in your lap.

Do not wait until you are ready to get off the bus before offering your seat to an elderly person.

Do not curb your dog on your neighbor's newly planted lawn.

Finally, do not arrive at your girlfriend's sweet sixteen party in torn jeans and a dirty T-shirt—to tell her how wonderful and informative this book is!

ENJOY!

Index